Lost at Sea

A Standalone Novel

Sail Away Series
Book Eight

Patricia Sands

Cover Design: Elizabeth Mackey
www.elizabethmackeygraphics.com

(p-v1)
Copyright © 2023 by Patricia Sands
All rights reserved.
ISBN 978-0-9861202-6-8

BOOKS BY PATRICIA SANDS

The Bridge Club

The Promise of Provence

Promises to Keep

I Promise You This

Drawing Lessons

The First Noël at the Villa des Violettes

A Season of Surprises at the Villa des Violettes

Lavender, Loss & Love at the Villa des Violettes

The Secrets We Hide

Lost At Sea

Lost at Sea
By Patricia Sands

PROLOGUE

For every family that is Italian going back several generations, this will sound familiar: It's a known fact that Italian women are passionate about everything, especially family, and they know that food is the essence of life.

From the day she was born in 1994, three strong women guided Stephanie Valentini's life: Bisnonna Paola, Nonna Bella, and Mamma Angela – her great-grandmother, grandmother, and mother. And for this the young woman was grateful. Among their many gifts to her, topmost were a love of cooking and a strong belief in herself.

After Stephanie (Stevie to her friends) received a business degree from the University of Toronto, she went to Florence for a year, to study at the Instituto Culinario, where she won both praise and awards for her *sugo,* the traditional Italian tomato sauce that slow-simmers to perfection.

This was followed by a six-month apprenticeship in a Venetian restaurant, which put a gold seal on what she had long known would be her life's passion. Cooking *all'italiana* was in her blood.

As her course was about to end, she received news her great-grandmother was seriously ill. She rushed back to Toronto and arrived in time to spend some moments with her beloved Paola, whose whispered last words to her were "*Sei la custode della nostra magia di famiglia...*" – her duty was to carry on the family magic.

The first thing Stevie did once she had stopped weeping was get a small tattoo of The Sun tarot card on the inside of her left wrist. Bisnonna Paola had read her cards since she was a toddler and The Sun was always there.

Stevie and her boyfriend, Benny Lombardi, moved into an apartment in the Little Italy neighbourhood of Toronto, where they had both grown up. She knew Paola had refused to consider Benny, her only boyfriend since high school, as anything more than an annoying friend, but dismissed the thought. Benny felt what Paola thought of him and swore to Stephanie that her great-grandmother regularly gave him the dreaded Italian *occhiatacce,* "stink-eye," behind her back. But Stevie thought they were in love and that, just on this one thing, Paola had been mistaken.

Stevie's life became routine as time went on, with

Paola's spirit a constant within her. She created magic in the kitchen of the restaurant her great-grandmother had started, waited tables in a jam, and basically ran every aspect of Cara Mia, with Nonna Bella taking on the role of guiding angel.

Reading was her outlet. Cooking was her passion. Benny was her sweetheart. He worked in advertising and handled the restaurant's social media. Except for StevieV's Pasta Party on TikTok. No one else could do that.

That was her life and she loved it.

At least she thought she did.

Until it all fell apart.

Now she lay on her bed, closed her eyes and, with Paola's spirit infusing every cell in her body, allowed her family's history to come to life in her head.

This history was where her future would begin.

1923 to 1945

Paola Valentini's journey was made in the aftermath of sorrow. It began deep in her homeland.

Since her birth in 1923 in her family's rustic stone cottage in a village near the ancient town of Marzabotta, the years had been hard but joyful. Then the second hateful world war had begun. What happened in September 1944 would forever burn in her heart and soul.

Paola's and Stefano's families had been neighbours

for generations. In their close-knit community, children and adults worked together to keep bees and raise silkworms, to grow and harvest grapes, figs and vegetables on the steep, terraced hillsides south of Bologna. There was just enough food to survive on and in a good year some to sell or barter. A few lucky children attended school until grade six before they were needed full-time to help.

It was hard work for little gain. But that was how life there had been for centuries. There had always been a sense of community, with everyone working to help each other. There had been joy in simple things: a wedding, a new baby, a good harvest, enough rain for the crops.

After the Great War, it had taken the village a long time to recover. Many men had perished, but there had been hope. Life went on. Most people were confident such devastation would never revisit them. Only a few were not so sure.

While they were still teenagers, Paola and Stefano promised their hearts to each other. They were soulmates who saw the glimmer of a rainbow in their future, in spite of life's daily challenges.

Then it happened. World War II. There was even more hardship, bringing unimagined loss and heartache. When the Germans moved in, their ruthless disregard for humanity made Stefano decide to join the Resistance.

Before he left for the shelter of the mountains, Stefano asked Paola to be his wife. She did not hesitate in saying yes. Aged eighteen, they were married in the village church. The next day he vanished into the forest to join with men of all ages to plan and carry out raids on the enemy.

For the next two years, Paola's family farm was secretly used as a safe house for wounded partisans and rescued Allied fighters. A cave deep under the stable, used to store food, provided an undetectable hiding place.

In May 1944, the local priest sent a young boy racing to tell Paola that her family must immediately go into hiding. All of her immediate family was working in fields, too far away to warn. Only a few cousins and neighbours were reachable. They went into the cellar under the stable and waited, barely able to breathe out of fear.

After three days, two of her young cousins cautiously left the cellar to investigate. Hours later, they came back, weeping and unable to speak, except to say the Germans had gone.

The horror that lay before Paola and her neighbours when they emerged was unimaginable. Unforgettable. There were bodies everywhere—scattered along the road to Marzabotta and in the town itself. Hundreds of townspeople, including young children, had been rounded up and slaughtered by German soldiers in revenge for an attack by the Resistance.

These few survivors who came out of the stable never recovered from the sight.

The Nazis were on the run but their cruelty could not be erased.

The following spring, after the Allies had vanquished the enemy, Paola spent her days working on reviving what was left of the garden.

One morning she wiped her eyes in disbelief as she watched Stefano limp up the laneway to the stable. It was the only structure that provided shelter now as the house was not more than a ruin. In a weakened condition herself, Paola moved as quickly as she could to fold her beloved husband into her arms before he collapsed. The love of her life had miraculously returned.

There were weeks of quiet rediscovery and healing, spiritually and bodily. Their love was strong, and slowly they created a plan to rebuild their lives now that all of their immediate relatives, except a few cousins, had been killed.

Their joy was immense when Paola discovered she was carrying their child. For the first time, they felt the promise of a better tomorrow. The summer weather had been good for the crops. Survival was a possibility. Their love gave them strength and hope.

In October, Stefano was in the forest with others cutting firewood when a large tree fell the wrong way, killing him instantly. Paola's cousin, Salvatore, delivered the devastating news.

February 1946

Under a star-filled sky, a frigid wind blew off the Atlantic. The prow of the enormous Greek ship, *Nea Hellas*, cut through the sea. The six decks gave it a regal appearance, but the passenger list did not represent anything close to royalty.

Towering black winter waves had slammed the ship

for more than a week after it left the calmer waters of the Mediterranean. The major crossing from Genoa to the new world was over. Now majestic icebergs floating south of Newfoundland brought passengers to the rails to gaze in wonder. The safe harbor of Halifax would be next.

The day the ship approached their final destination, Paola was on the lowest deck, gripping the rail with gloved hands, tears frozen to her cheeks. Her cousin Salvatore leaned toward her and said, "Canada".

Their eyes met and Paola's lips formed the words "*una nuova casa*". Salvatore nodded with a smile. He slipped his arm around her shoulder and pulled her close, in a comforting hug. "*Sì,*" he said.

A new home awaited them.

Paola had left behind everything she knew and loved. The baby due in two months was all she could take with her. She had no option but to begin again, to build a life for herself and her baby. Stefano's baby. Her Stefano.

Their closest remaining relatives had immigrated to Toronto before the war. Now those cousins were sponsors for Paola and Salvatore. They were waiting to welcome the newcomers with loving arms to Toronto's caring Little Italy neighborhood.

1946–2021

Shortly after the birth of her daughter, Isabella, in April 1946, Paola began making her *sugo*, a simple, delicious tomato sauce, in the cramped kitchen of her cousins' small apartment. The recipe had been passed down through many generations and countless gallons had been cooked on the family's wood-burning stove in the small cottage in the hills south of Bologna.

She began to sell the sauce to friends and neighbours, and it was not long before word spread. Every day, a steady stream of people came to buy a jar. Then, the whisper started going around that the sauce had magical powers. The Little Italy neighbourhood became the happiest place to live in the burgeoning city. Paola knew her *sugo* was the reason, but kept that to herself.

She decided to add fresh pasta to her repertoire, standard daily fare at home in Italy. It was also a winner. Demand grew to the point that her cousins pitched in with packaging and cleaning up. Paola supplied the Italian groceteria that had opened on the ground floor with both pasta and sauce.

Eventually, all the extended family moved into a rambling Victorian house on a quiet side street. When the store downstairs from their original apartment came up for sale, they pooled their savings and bought it. With help from cousins working in construction, they turned their old apartment into a kitchen and the storefront into a restaurant. The family trattoria, Cara Mia, was born.

Paola never remarried and was still in charge of the kitchen when Isabella married Luigi Valentini, a distant cousin. A year later their son, Angelo, was born. Each generation worked alongside Paola.

Many years later, Angelo and his wife, Angela, named their first child Stephanie to honor Paola's lost love. She was delighted and formed a strong bond with her new great-granddaughter. She loved Stephanie with all her heart and knew the first time she carried her into Cara Mia's kitchen, as an infant, that the magical family *all'italiana* cooking genes had been passed on. She could feel it in her soul. As her mother had with her and hers before that and so on in the family for as long as their history was known.

Stephanie began stirring pots in the kitchen with her beloved Bisnonna and Nonna Bella as soon as she could reach the stove. The cooking gene had skipped one generation. Her father Angelo and mother Angela——The Angels as they became known——instead looked after the business side of things as the successful trattoria grew out of that original crowded kitchen.

As a little girl, Stephanie would sit on her Bisnonna's knee and listen to stories about her childhood in Italy. Stephanie always felt wrapped in a warm glow whenever they were together. In her teenage years, if she was troubled about something, Paola still would read Tarot cards to get to the cause of the problem. She swore they were the storybook of one's life. "The mirror to the soul." "*Il libro di fiabe della nostra vita. Lo specchio dell'anima.*"

Paola spoke only Italian to her from the time Stephanie was born, She never called Stephanie by her nickname and would tuck The Sun tarot card under her pillow each evening, whispering in Italian, "The Sun will shine joy and happiness into your life, *cara mia*. Even when clouds surround you."

When Stephanie was ten, Bisnonna Paola taught her how to make the delicious tomato sauce, the *sugo*, the trattoria was famous for, and Stephanie showed great talent for cooking. By now, Paolo was eighty-one. Nonna Isabella, sixty-three, ruled the kitchen under the watchful eye of Paola. Nonno Luigi handled the business accounts until his early passing when Stevie was thirteen.

Luigi had trained Angelo well and, after his father passed, he took over the administrative part of the business. Angela had found her true calling greeting customers, writing menus, organizing supplies, and keeping the décor fresh. The trattoria flourished.

Stephanie's star in the kitchen grew brighter each year. None of her family called her Stevie but she loved them all with a fierce loyalty. Family was everything. The restaurant was her destiny.

Paola always lovingly told her great-granddaughter how proud she was of her, and how proud she knew Stefano would be that she carried his name and his fiery spirit. She would also whisper to Stephanie how she must go to Italy to find her true love, her soulmate. "Stefano's spirit is waiting for you there, *cara mia*. You will go to our village and find it." Stevie would nod and kiss her cheek and pretend to agree. You never disagreed with Bisnonna.

The family traveled to Italy twice together. The visits were emotional and memorable but Stephanie had not felt any spirit calling to her. Bisnonna Paola had patted her hand, saying, "*Aspetta che sia il momento giusto. Lo saprai.*" "Wait until the time is right. You will know."

These thoughts brought Stephanie full circle back to where she had lain on her bed and time-travelled from the beginning of Paola's journey.

May 2021

Il tempismo è tutto. Timing is everything, Nonna Bella would say.

And then Kim's phone call happened.

When Stevie decided she had to take the call from her best friend, there were three things she knew for certain.

Her heart was broken.

She was exhausted.

If she never saw another drop of tomato sauce it would be too soon.

For the last three days, she still took calls from her parents and Nonna Bella, of course, but that was it. And they all knew chatting was not on the table right now.

Had it not been for Caller ID, she wouldn't have answered. But as soon as IT'S ME! flashed on the screen, she picked up after the first ring. When Kimberly Lake, her bestie since kindergarten, was on the line there was no option.

Stephanie's world had collapsed, and Kim had no idea. Now all that crap was going to have to be put into words.

"Hey Kimster," Stevie muttered. But she felt a flicker of happiness knowing her friend was on the other end of the line. "You are just what the doctor ordered. What exotic port are you in today?"

"Never mind me. I've texted, emailed and left voice-mail for the last three days. You've not replied to any of them!" Kim's normally calm voice had a definite rattle to it. "What's going on? Are you ok?"

"Sorry. Truly sorry. I knew you had a busy schedule, and when the shit hit the fan here, I went dark. Stayed offline with the covers over my head."

"I knew something was wrong when I didn't see a post from you on TikTok," Kim said. "How could there not be my daily dose of the Pasta Party?"

Stevie grunted. She knew she should have forced herself to keep up TikTok. With such a huge following, someone was bound to notice her absence.

"Start at the beginning please." Kim's tone reflected her concern. "I'm sitting on the upper deck looking out at the stunning Amalfi coast and planning how I'm going to survive the next month. I need some of your energy and good karma, but it doesn't sound like there's much available at the moment. Talk to me."

One thing Stephanie and Kimberly shared was a wicked sense of humor and an abundance of positivity. When the supply was low with one of them, it was quickly replenished by a conversation——or sometimes just a word——with the other.

Stevie blew out a long sigh and stretched her entire five feet two inches. She put the phone on speaker and walked over to the floor-to-ceiling window of her shoe-box-sized condo. The fact that the day was glorious made no impression.

"Spill," Kim ordered, but with the warmth of their friendship putting love in the command.

And Stevie prepared to spill. Every last ugly detail.

If anyone could come up with a way to help her feel better it would be Kim.

And Stevie was right about that, as she was about to discover.

CHAPTER 1

THE WORST OF IT

"Ok, here's the worst first. Benny's left me."

There was silence on the other end before a long "Whaaaaa?" in a voice that was low and full of disbelief. "Left you? What does that mean? You've been together for thirteen years––since Grade 10. He left you? As in gone, broken up, not together anymore?"

"Exactly. All of that."

Stephanie was not one for public displays of emotion, so there were none of the usual tears and sobs of a young woman dumped by her high-school sweetheart; someone who had been her constant companion, with whom she'd planned every detail of their wedding, not to mention their ongoing life together.

There had been weeping and gnashing of teeth and swearing and throwing things around, but all in the privacy of her own space. Now she was past that. Crying had never been her thing. And no one knew that better than Kim.

"What the hell happened?"

Staring vacantly out the window, ignoring the spectacular view over rooftops and between downtown high-rises right through to a glistening Lake Ontario, Stevie replied, "Here's the short version. He left last week for what he said was a two-day business trip to Montreal. Before his flight home, he tested positive for Covid so had to stay for five days. At least that was the story. He said he wasn't symptomatic. He came home three days ago."

She closed her eyes and paused for a moment, blowing out another big breath.

"When I dragged myself in from the restaurant that night he had his bags packed at the door. He said he would always care for me and hoped we could be friends. Then he said he was in love with Guido and moving in with him. They'd bought a place together in Montreal. Badda bing, badda boom."

"Stevie. I think I need to hang up and call you again. This can't be real."

"It's real."

"You were meant for each other."

"Apparently not."

"You've never had any problems."

"Well, I guess we have."

"And Guido? His personal trainer? Your personal trainer?"

"Um, yeah. That part."

"They're in love?"

"Apparently so."

As can happen comfortably between such friends, they stayed quiet for a moment.

Then Stevie heard Kim sniffle and knew she was crying. She expected that. As calm, cool and collected as Stevie was, Kim wore her heart on her sleeve and her emotions rested just below the surface of her porcelain skin. She cried watching game shows. She was kindness personified and the first to offer help in whatever situation. And whip-smart. Stevie loved her for all of that.

Kim blew her nose and apologized. "Let's FaceTime. I need to see you. I'll call you right back."

Stephanie took a quick look in the mirror and tucked her auburn curls behind her ears. She didn't need to worry about mascara trails down her cheeks. She hadn't worn any for days. And that was a tell-tale sign. Stevie Valentini never stepped out the door without wearing mascara. Make-up was not a big thing with her, except for mascara.

Whatever—she and Kim had definitely seen each other at their worst through twenty-four years.

As soon as they could see each other on their phone screens, Kim shook her head and wiped the tears that were continuing to fall.

Stephanie pursed her lips, raised her eyebrows and nodded. "Crazy or what? I've cried all my tears and you know I'm not a crier. I've also thrown around pretty much everything that wasn't nailed down here. I'm done."

"There was no w-w-warning?" Kim stuttered.

Stephanie shrugged. "What can I say? When you've been together for so many years like we have, it isn't all sweetness and romance. And the last two of the five years we've lived together have been pretty much under lock-down, so there's that too."

Kim nodded. "Not to mention the fact that you've basically lived at the restaurant preparing take-out meals for the past two years."

"And arriving home at midnight, tired, reeking of garlic," Stephanie added, her voice tired, tinged with remorse.

The pandemic had changed everything.

"And Benny was stressed out a lot during the last two years because his studies were all online. We weren't exactly the best company."

Benny had completed an MBA during lockdown and was working with a high-pressure advertising company. Keeping fit was his outlet. He was a Peleton addict all year round and played hockey and golf as often as possible before everything was locked down. That was his life and he loved it.

Despite their busy schedules they always made time for each other. They both loved to laugh and took life's challenges in stride. Or so Stevie thought.

Kim frowned. "The past two years have been tough, you're right about that. But you, and Benny, and Guido ——I can't get my head around that. I am so, so, sorry you have been hurt like this. I wish I could come over to your place this minute."

Stephanie stared back at her, her dark eyes clear. "Me too. Let's not talk about it now though. I'm not fine but I'm in control——for now anyway. As Bisnonna always said, "*Non preoccuparti, sii felice*" and Nonna Bella has never stopped reminding me.

Kim chuckled. "The Italian version of don't worry, be happy. How many times have I heard that at your place. From three of the most upbeat women I've ever known. I'm so glad I got to be close to your family."

Her eyes misted over and she looked away. "I miss Bisnonna even though she's been gone—, what? eight years now."

Stephanie nodded. "Yup, exactly. She was ninety-one and still sharp as a tack. Not a day without a tarot reading. But she was increasingly ticked that darn arthritis prevented her from doing practically everything. She just kind of said *basta*! one morning and lay down and died. She definitely had enough, but her spirit has stayed with all of us."

Stephanie turned away from the window and wandered back to her kitchen, where she sat at the counter. It was time to change the conversation

"But enough about me," she said. "You're looking out at the Isle of Capri? Turn your phone around, girl-friend! Let me see!"

Kim held her phone steady and the stunning iconic landscape of Capri appeared on the screen. A steep cliff rose from the sea to reach lush, terraced gardens and beyond to a forested hilltop. Turquoise water in multi shades lapped at the entrance to a deep cave. With a bright blue sky as background, large jagged rocks jutted out of the water, with tourist boats bobbing around them.

"Aha, the Faraglioni rocks!" Stephanie squealed. "I know them. We went to the Amalfi coast on one of our family trips. "What perfect timing for you to call me!"

"Ha! I was pretty sure you would recognize them," Kim replied. One of the advantages to being on a smaller ship like this is that we can get so much closer than the big cruise ships."

"What a life you are having! Woohoo!"

"Yeah, big whoop." Kim sounded less than enthusiastic.

"Ok. Now it's my turn to ask what's going on? That was hardly an excited tone. What's up with you and your shipboard adventures? How are sales going? Spill!"

Kim was a jewelry designer. For a few years she had a small shop in Toronto's upscale Yorkville neighborhood — until Covid struck and the lockdown began. From then on, she worked out of her studio in a Victorian townhouse on a street off Avenue Road, and built a steady online business. She'd also occasionally hired staff to run a pop-up shop on a ship belonging to an exclusive cruise line.

"Y'know, I feel sort of bad admitting that I really didn't mind being locked down so much," Kim said.

Stephanie nodded. "Yeah, I could see you loved being by yourself. Unbelievable as it was at first."

"And you were shocked I was not worrying about who my next date was going to be."

"That part was totally unbelievable."

Kim blew a raspberry. "Haha. Well, I finally wised up to the fact I had been wasting a whole lot of time on a long list of losers. Oh——wait——then I realized perhaps I was the loser!"

"No way!"

"Seriously. I may just be too picky. But when I

walked away from the dating scene, the lockdown became my most creative time. That's why I have all this jewelry to sell now." She flashed her brilliant smile, then she frowned and her eyes filled with tears.

"Hey! I thought you were looking forward to taking care of your shipboard shop," Stevie said. "You didn't sound upset about it the last few times we talked."

"I was trying to pull up my big girl panties and deal with the issues that were bothering me. Besides I didn't want to complain to you when I knew how hard you all were working to keep the restaurant going."

Stephanie had heard all about the couple who had been working for Kim on the *Dream Maker*. Things had been going just fine, but after Covid hit everything turned upside down there. They got stuck in lockdown on board for months, quit as soon as they could disembark, and never wanted to go back once cruising started again.

The shop had stayed shuttered for a while with a substantial amount of stock.

As a last resort, Kim had gone on the ship the previous month to manage things on her own. "How hard can it be?" she had asked Stevie at the time.

"I can't do this!" Kim wailed now. "It's too much for one person and I'm committed to the next trip. I can't bail. But I can't find any staff. I'm too busy to even look properly."

Stephanie stared at the screen but said nothing.

"I don't know how I can fix this," Kim continued. "I guess I'll just have to suck it up and get through it. I can do it but it won't be fun. And what's the point of being on a luxury cruise like this if it isn't fun? Crazy, huh?"

"Yeah, crazy all right. When I read the itinerary for last month I couldn't believe how awesome the trip is ——thirty days, ten ports and a Michelin-starred restaurant meal at each one. Sounds like a dream to me."

"No dream if you are working like a fiend every day and too exhausted to enjoy it. Trust me! Oh—and the Michelin-star restos are not for the crew. Just sayin'. I'm all for the small local places anyway."

Stephanie fought back a grin. "Would it be more fun if your bestie was there with you?"

Kim snorted. "Duh! Of course. It would make all the difference in the world."

"And we would find time to have fun. We've always been good at that! I'm tempted!"

"Hey, now I'm feeling guilty for putting this on you. But don't talk nonsense. You have your own responsibilities there with the restaurant."

"Funny you should mention that. The Angels announced they have decided to shut down for three months starting at the end of this week." She always referred to her parents by their first names or by the joint tag they had been given when they first married.

A piercing scream came through the phone. "Shut up! Don't tease me! Seriously?"

Stephanie nodded and grinned. "Decided yesterday. After Benny took a hike, they looked at me and made an executive decision. Angela aptly summed it up by saying we are all totally burnt out. We made it through the worst of the lockdowns with our takeout service, and we can afford to simply shut down for a while. She said that I needed a break from everything and so did they."

"And how did Nonna Bella react to that? I know she still rules," Kim asked.

"In fact, I'm told it was Nonna who first made the suggestion."

"Oh my geeeee!" Kim shouted. "What could be a better break than coming along with me next month? Well, actually we will be back in Barcelona in ten days, have a week in port and then head out on our foodie tour. Please say you are coming. Please, please, please! Does that sound like begging? Because it is!"

They stared at each other, looking like they were about to burst.

"This is unbelievable! A dream come true for me and it might be for you too! Just what the doctor ordered," Kim said, her green eyes sparkling.

"Not so fast, my BFF. I'm not certain what kind of company I will be. I have to tell you I'm hurting. I'm confused——lost——I don't know what I want or where I'm headed. So, a warning. I'm not in a good space."

"Then who better to hang with than me? Haven't we been through everything together since forever? How many times have you held my hand?" Kim asked, flipping her long ash blond hair over her shoulder and rolling her eyes.

She was right about that, Stephanie thought. There had been a few disastrous love affairs, after a happy early marriage which ended prematurely in a fatal car accident.

Stephanie had felt that Kim and her husband,

Johnny, were living the ultimate love story, young as they were. They had met at art college and fallen quickly and tenderly for each other.

Their future looked bright, all the stars appeared to be aligned, when they married at age twenty-one. As chaotic as Stephanie and Benny's lives were then, she always harboured a hope that one day they would share the same kind of love. That hadn't happened.

Kim and Johnny had planned to start a family, but not until their careers were in place. A year and a half after they married, Johnny was killed in a head-on collision with a drunk driver. Stephanie had never forgotten the piercing grief of that tragedy.

But Kim had faced the reality squarely. In the years following, she often said how the love they had shared in their short time together prepared her for the worst that life had dealt her.

After two years of grieving, Kim had started dating. She knew she could never replace Johnny, but he had shown her how wonderful true love could be. She believed she would find it again. But the search for it was not so wonderful, Kim eventually realized. And Stephanie had been Kim's support through it all.

There had been a period of online dating that provided either jaw-droppingly horrible or hilarious experiences. Kim never did anything halfway. There were days she had three dates with different guys——lunch, afternoon coffee or drink, and dinner.

When Stephanie and Kim were hanging out together, Kim would sometimes log onto her dating site and they would check out the bios of guys who were "nudging" her or sending a "wink" They would erupt in gales of laughter as they read descriptions that did not remotely match the photos. Kim also had colorful stories about dates where the man turned up looking fifteen years older and with considerably less hair and many more pounds than in their photo.

Kim eventually got fed up, and for the past two years, with the help of Covid and lockdowns, she had taken a pass on dating. She focused on her jewelry collections where she achieved stunning results. Through skillful searches at estate sales, she had acquired an impressive number of vintage broaches, bracelets and necklaces. The style of her own line was minimalist, strictly silver, and had received several awards. And now there was beading, her new addiction.

"It's my turn, Stevie-boo. My shoulder is waiting for you. Get your butt across the Atlantic and come on the adventure of our lives together. We can make it fun."

"I won't be the life of the party," Stephanie warned. "But then I never was."

"You won't have to be. We will work hard when we have to and relax when we can. We can slip away to explore the amazing places we will be visiting since we get ample time off in each port. Check out the itinerary again. I'll send you the link right now."

"How do I apply to work on the ship? Won't that take a while?"

Kim was grinning from ear to ear now. "Nooo! You will be working for me, not the cruise company. So I can hire you immediately, and they will approve it."

"Fantastic! But—full disclosure—I'll be a tourist and

a jewelry salesperson. Don't tell anyone that I cook. *Capiche?* I will just be Stephanie to everyone and not Stevie, except to you in private, okay? And I am definitely not interested in meeting any guys. Zero!"

She stopped and blinked. "Was that bossy?"

"Not at all. Understood. This is your escape," Kim said. "Besides, most of the passengers are seniors who are more interested in gourmet food and fine wine than *amore*. There are some great people on staff. Lots of the crew are so involved in their own affairs and intrigues, they won't pay any attention to us. There's a real hierarchy on a ship, kinda like the *Upstairs, Downstairs* series our parents watched. Remember?"

"Sounds like I have a lot to learn about this cruising life. But I'm up for the challenge. You may have just rescued me, Kimski!"

CHAPTER 2

BARCELONA JUNE 1/21

Two weeks after that phone call, and a few subsequent conversations about Benny, often tear-filled (by Kim), Stephanie boarded a direct overnight flight from Toronto to Barcelona. She arrived mid-morning and made her way to the quaint hotel they had booked for two nights, where Kim was waiting in the lobby.

"We will be on the ship for a month, so let's enjoy some different surroundings while we can," Kim had suggested in their last phone call.

After Stephanie freshened up in a small room and left her luggage there, they set off on a walking tour detailed in a map Kim had picked up in the lobby. Now they sat outside at a tapas bar on a narrow alleyway just off the famous tree-lined pedestrian boulevard, Las Ramblas, in the heart of the city.

Beads of water dripped off the pitcher of icy sangria as Kim refilled their glasses. A waiter placed a plate of tapas on the table: olives, Manchego cheese and the local ham.

"You weren't joking when you warned me it was hot. And this is just May!" Stephanie fanned her face with a silk fan she had purchased as they strolled. "These things are extremely effective. I'm surprised."

"Now you know why they've been used here for hundreds of years!" Kim said. "They're not just for tourists. After we cool off, we'll pop down the street to the incredible market, La Boqueria. I purposely had us stop here so we won't be so tempted to eat when we get there. You will see why."

Stevie laughed. "I have a feeling I'll be tempted to eat everywhere here, from what I've seen of food so far." Then she yawned. "And, needless to say, my body clock is totally out of whack so I may need a nap soon."

"For sure," Kim agreed. "Our room should be ready in an hour or so. I figured you would want to crash for a while. Then we have a reservation at nine o'clock for dinner just down the street from our hotel. The food is good but what's really important is that the flamenco is outstanding. You're gonna love it!"

"Okay, let's hit the market now or you may have to carry me back to the hotel."

Kim had been right, the Mercado La Boqueria was incredible, filled with spectacular displays of fruit, vegetables, meat, cheeses, oils, wines, and, most impressive of all, seafood. There were free samples of everything and the ambience was electric with spirited voices, lively music and the entertaining banter of vendors enticing customers.

Stephanie's cooking persona kicked in and her pulse quickened as they strolled the aisles in the remarkable art nouveau building. "I can't believe the selection and variety of food on offer. And all these great areas to eat. I could spend days in here! And I might be feeling the urge to shop and cook. How could I not?"

Before Kim could respond, Stephanie answered her own question. "But I will not. To be clear, I'm not lifting a spoon to pot on this trip."

Kim grinned. "That's what you said and not why you are here, but I knew you would love this anyway! It's been operating since 1836, and there are over two hundred vendors. Someone described it to me as the beating heart of the city."

They stopped at one of many stands selling colorful cups overflowing with fresh fruit.

"Mmmm, so refreshing and such flavor," was all Stephanie could murmur repeatedly as they sat on stools at the busy bar.

Kim agreed. "I've never seen fruit displayed like this at home, have you?"

Stephanie shook her head and then leaned over and gave Kim a hug. "It's amazing.! And overwhelming! I'm in Barcelona and it's all thanks to you!"

They high-fived and laughed.

"When I was at cooking school in Italy, we went on two field trips. One to Lyon and the other to San Sebastián. I planned to come here when I was interning in Venice but never made it. That was the year Bisnonna died."

"I remember you rushed back home just a few days

before she passed," Kim recalled. "What a force of power she was. I still miss her and I know you do."

"No kidding," Stevie agreed. "I've been thinking a lot about her since my life turned into crazy town. She set such an example of strength and determination. I learned so much from her. What she experienced during and after WW2 was unimaginable. I have nothing to complain about and I know it! Now I've got to dig deep and get my act together."

Kim reached for Stephanie's hand. "And why wouldn't you? You've had quite a shock and it's going to take a while to put everything in perspective. But there are better days ahead. We both realize that. Baby steps, my friend, baby steps."

They exchanged knowing looks and walked back to the hotel arm in arm. There was time for a quick shower and a two-hour nap for Stephanie before they headed out to dinner.

"Jet lag be damned," Stephanie declared. "I'm not going to miss this chance of eating in someone else's restaurant!"

CHAPTER 3

FABULOUS FLAMENCO

The lights in the narrow dining room were dramatically dimmed, creating a warm and intimate atmosphere. Its terra cotta floor tiles, wooden beams, and stucco walls hung with cast iron lanterns, provided just the right setting for the flamenco performance.

Stephanie and Kim had just finished eating when they heard the first impassioned chords of a lone flamenco guitar. They hadn't noticed the guitarist take a seat on a platform at one side of the room.

Four men strolled out and stood behind the guitarist. They began to clap rhythmically as the spotlight moved to shine on a woman in a ruffled yellow dress standing still and silent.

After a few moments, the woman clapped her hands to the beat, stomped her feet and began a passionate dance of dips and whirls accompanied by delicate hand and arm movements. Her jet-black hair was pulled back in a dramatic chignon to allow her emotional facial expressions to show.

A haunting, melancholic male voice sang out, and the room was filled with a sensual kaleidoscope of emotions. There were intense calls including "Olé" and "Que toma!" from the audience.

Stephanie and Kim were both enchanted. Their eyes never left the stage until the song ended. Then the audience clapped wildly and shouted "Bravo! Brava!"

"Hooooooleeeeee!" Kim breathed out.

Stephanie nodded, wide-eyed.

They both took a long sip of wine.

"I may need to take my fan out again," Stephanie said. "That was hot!"

"Steaming hot," Kim agreed. "I've only been here once before, but I haven't stopped thinking about when I could get back. I'm so glad you saw that with me. Was it awesome or what?"

"So much emotion! The combination of the guitar, the voices and the dance was like this explosion of the deepest feelings imaginable," Stephanie said. "I've never seen anything like it."

Next a single male appeared, dressed in tight, black shirt and pants. Without any accompaniment, he danced alone, stamping a percussive rhythm with his shoes. "That's called *zapateado*," Kim said afterward. "I looked it up after the first show I saw."

"Hypnotic," Stephanie gasped.

After a brief intermission, the show continued with four women performing a seamlessly coordinated dance. Two of them used fans to dramatic effect, and the other two played castanets. The finale of the show was two fiery dances by a young man and woman, whose grace and erotic physicality brought everyone in the room to their feet, cheering.

"Breathless," Kim said. "I'm simply breathless."

Stephanie shakily got to her feet. "For someone who thought she was void of emotion, I can't believe the impact of those performances. I'm exhausted."

"That was something else," Kim agreed. "Add your jet lag to that, and I guess you are ready to fall over. Let's get back to the hotel."

"I've been stifling yawns for the last hour and may fall over at any moment. But I wouldn't have missed that for anything."

As they walked along quiet streets back to the hotel, they could not stop talking about the evening.

"The dinner was the best *pollo al ajillo* I've ever tasted," Stephanie said. "The Spanish have a way with garlic and chicken that I haven't found matched in any other cuisine."

"And those patatas bravas were the best!" Kim added. "I've tried to make them but never quite get it right."

"Again," Stephanie said, "it's all about the garlic! But——that show! Probably the best entertainment I've seen. Flamenco live is an experience I never expected—"

"Pure art. In every way." Kim yawned. Within minutes of reaching their hotel room, Stephanie was in bed. As she was dozing off, memories of Benny saying he was leaving rushed into her head: his suitcases and duffel bags in the front hall of their apartment; him standing by the window in the living room, waiting for her; his words; her shock and disbelief.

She lay staring at the ceiling for what felt like forever before she succumbed to the exhaustion that had been building for weeks.

Their next two days in Barcelona were filled with visits to as many of the amazing tourist attractions as they could cram in. Hours were consumed with a Gaudi tour that culminated at the spectacular Sagrada Familia. As non-religious as Stevie was, she could not help being over-whelmed by the uniquely creative beauty Gaudi had designed. She was intrigued by the fascinating story of how it had continued to be built ever since his death in 1926.

There was no question of her answer when Kim asked if she wanted to catch another flamenco show.

They taxied to the beach and, after arranging for the driver to collect them later, just made it in time to have a delicious paella dinner. The driver picked them up as promised and dropped them at a hole in the wall where their hotel concierge had managed to secure them seats for the late evening flamenco show. It was as rousing and spectacular as the previous night's performance.

"I may never need another man in my life," Stephanie gushed afterward. "I'm in love with Barcelona!"

Kim laughed and gave her a hug. "You've forgotten how fabulous travel in Europe is. We're just getting started, girlfriend. This is simply your first new crush."

CHAPTER 4

ON BOARD

The next morning, after taking Covid tests just down the street from their hotel, they made their way to the ship. Both tests were negative.

"It will be nice when we don't have to bother with this anymore," Stephanie said.

"For sure," Kim agreed. "And, by the way, all the passengers and crew on *Dream Maker* have to show proof of vaccination and negative tests. The good news is that makes masking unnecessary."

As the taxi wound through the maze of terminals and cargo docks at the Port de Barcelona, Stephanie was surprised at the new development she was seeing. Their driver explained in excellent English that the port had been cleverly redeveloped for the 1992 Olympics to merge it with the city. It was now a tourist attraction in its own right, with cafés and shopping. In the heart of it, the old, fourteenth-century Port Vell was now a harbour for yachts and cruise ships, and when she spotted them, Kim pointed out the masts of the *Dream Maker*.

Stephanie had seen photos and videos of the ship before she left Toronto, but they did not compare to the breathtaking reality of the sleek white hull with five tall masts that reached skyward. She gasped before she was able to murmur, "What a beauty."

"Just wait until the sails are unfurled," Kim said. "It's magical."

Two burly security guards were at the foot of the gangway and greeted the women in Catalan, which sounded charming to their ears. Kim and Stephanie showed their identity passes and boarded, with Kim nudging Stephanie's ribs and murmuring under her breath, "Hoooola, amigos," after they had passed them.

Stephanie gave her a sideways look. "Kim, I'm serious about not getting hung up on any guys on this trip. Stop salivating!"

"I'm simply looking and expressing appreciation for the eye candy, honest! You should too."

At the top of the gangway, a shortish man with curly light brown hair and a taller dark-haired woman, both wearing smart white marine-style uniforms grinned at them. Kim explained that the cruise line's security had called the ship earlier to alert them to their arrival. Appearing to be in their thirties, they offered salutes and then fist bumps as Kim introduced Stephanie.

"Meet Staff Captain Katherine Wilson and our cruise director, First Officer Liam O'Sullivan," Kim said. Stevie noted they had different colored stripes on their epaulets and each had four. She knew she had a lot to learn about life on the ship, and figured this was the first clue she needed to solve.

"Stephanie, we're delighted to welcome you aboard!" Liam said, his thick Irish accent causing her to grin. Katherine beamed in agreement.

"Kim has told us that you are lifelong friends" Katherine said. "How cool to work this cruise together. You're going to love it."

She asked a few polite questions about their stay in Barcelona, and then they all walked through the open French doors into the main salon.

Stephanie hoped her expression didn't make her look too overwhelmed. Kim chuckled. "It's pretty awesome, isn't it? I had the same reaction the first time I came aboard."

Smiling proudly, Katherine said, "That's pretty much standard."

"It's like a designer showroom——in all the best ways," Stephanie exclaimed.

Leather couches and chairs in varying shades of cream and rust, gleaming wood floors and elegant lighting, polished teak desks, tables and a long reception counter on one side all offered an instantly welcoming ambiance. Grand floral arrangements in peach and cream were placed in all the right spots.

"Once you have settled in your quarters, have Kim bring you up to the bridge to meet Captain Keeling and some of the other officers," Katherine said. "Take your time. Today is pretty quiet until the welcome cocktail party for the crew, staff and officers at five this afternoon.

Stephanie noticed Kim and Liam were already having a giggle about something.

"Kim, m'dear," Liam said, a sparkle in his bright blue

eyes. "I hope you warned Stephanie about the crazy cocktail parties our crew has."

Kim chuckled. "Don't worry, I've given her a
complete rundown on all of the shenanigans to expect
under your careful supervision."

"Who has more fun than we do?" he replied.

Katherine rolled her eyes. "And *always* professional,
Liam. Correct?"

Liam snapped to attention and smartly saluted her.
"Aye, aye, Ma'am!"

Stephanie had to stifle her laughter at his comedic
expression. There was no question in her mind Liam
would be a force to be reckoned with. Katherine waved
and headed down a corridor.

"See you later!" Katherine called back, unable to
disguise a chuckle.

During a tour of the main level led by Liam,
Stephanie continued to be impressed. The ship had a
cozy library with well-stocked shelves and broad
windows, an inviting bar, and an elegant dining room
that led to a patio on the foredeck.

Liam's non-stop commentary was pure entertainment. He babbled on until they came to a bank of
elevators.

"Righty-ho! We will part ways here, my treasures! I
look forward to seeing you later. Cheerio!"

Kim pressed button number three. When the
elevator stopped, they stepped into a narrow hallway
lined with polished teak doors and gleaming brass
hardware.

"We got lucky, Stevie. Because we agreed to share a

room, we actually scored one on the same floor as the officers. Normally we would each be in a tiny room on the floor above the crew quarters, which are in the lowest level. We qualify as staff which is a level above crew, but there was one double room available on the officers' level, so they gave it to us."

Stephanie smiled. "It could be a good omen."

After fifteen minutes of unpacking and organizing, they congratulated each other on keeping to the limited clothing list they had worked on.

"You were not exaggerating about the skimpy closets," Stevie exclaimed. "Good thing I'm not a clothes horse and you have always been the queen of co-ordinating your wardrobe. Your advice was bang on. I'm impressed."

They settled into the two comfortable upholstered chairs facing the sliding glass doors, which opened to a Juliette balcony. On the small table between them sat an ice bucket with a split of champagne that Stevie had picked up at the duty-free shop in the Toronto airport.

"I figured we should start our voyage in style," she said.

They clinked their glasses and Kim toasted, "To you and to me wherever we roam—um—I can't remember the rest of it."

"Classic Kim! But that sounded good to me. Our adventure is now officially under way! Did you have time to look at the links I sent you the other day about hiking trails in all of our ports?"

"I did and I forwarded them to Liam. He's better than Google when it comes to that sort of information.

He's been working on this cruise itinerary for ten years and has all the inside tips. He said he would put together a schedule for us."

"I liked him a lot," Stephanie said, "—and all of the Irish blarney that sounds so hilarious in his accent. He's got a good sense of humor."

"He loves his job and the passengers all love him. He can work his magic on the most cantankerous of personalities. But when he is off duty, look out! He's a force to be reckoned with and can talk you into doing the unthinkable ——within reason, of course—Well, most of the time."

They chatted a while longer as Kim described some of the other crew on board. "But never mind. You will start to meet them all today and see for yourself. Let's go up on the bridge now. It's stunning."

The elevator brought them to the top level of the ship, where they walked into a vast open space surrounded by windows. A massive panel filled with monitors, maps, dials and control levers stretched across the front under the windows that wrapped around the room. Two padded elevated chairs faced this with a bank of controls between them.

"Hello *Star Trek*," Stephanie murmured.

Captain James Keeling greeted them effusively. "Welcome aboard, Kim's friend Stephanie. We're delighted you are joining us and guarantee you are going to love the experience. Feel free to visit us up here any time."

They hung around briefly, meeting a few other officers and technicians and then headed down to the main level, to Kim's shop.

"Oh man!" Stephanie exclaimed as they walked away. "Talk about impressive! How amazing to have all that technology! Times have certainly changed since a sailor relied on the ship's wheel, rudder, compass and the stars."

Unlocking the sliding front windows, Kim gave Stephanie a quick rundown of how things worked in the shop. First, she slid open a panel that allowed them to move into the middle of the u-shaped counter.

"We stay in here and have these stools to sit on if we get tired. It feels a bit like a bar. Then we put the pieces on top as people want to look at them."

She slid out the velvet covered shelves underneath the glass counters.

The jewelry was divided into three sections. First were Kim's silver creations which consisted of rings, bracelets and necklaces, all her own designs. Second were the vintage pieces she searched for sporadically at markets and auctions and kept until she had a significant collection to show. Third were the beaded pieces she had begun making after attending several beading workshops before Covid hit.

"Kimski! I'm overwhelmed with all of these. The pieces are beautiful and so different!"

"Beading is my new passion, as you know. I can't get enough of it," Kim admitted. "It's become somewhat of an addiction, and I brought supplies with me to work on when I was alone. So, I have some new pieces almost finished to add."

"The colors are so yummy. I can almost taste them! I

want to buy them all! Wow! It's going to be so much fun watching people shop here."

"First thing tomorrow morning – and I do mean first thing, like six o'clock – we will set up the displays and be good to go. There's some polishing and shining to do. Passengers begin boarding at eight, and we'll open for business soon after we set sail in the afternoon"

"Aye, aye, ma'am!" Stephanie saluted. Kim snorted and screwed her face into a comical grimace.

"Okay. That's the first and last time I'll do that," Stephanie promised.

"Darn right. Let's go shower and change for the cocktail party. There's a fabulous buffet spread included, so that takes care of dinner. It'll be so much fun. You will meet the entire crew, and from what I've heard that is quite unusual on our other ships. But the captain is a big believer in treating everyone with respect whether they clean bathrooms or keep the ship afloat."

"Sounds cool. Good work environment."

The party was all Kim had promised. The buffet was split into six food stations with hot and cold choices, an astounding display of seafood that looked like a work of art including sushi and sashimi, and a dessert table that was impossible to resist. The bar was serving the most colorful and creative cocktails Stevie had ever seen.

"I'm almost relieved to see there's very little Italian food here," she commented to Kim.

"Just wait until we hit the Italian ports. They save it

until then for effect," Kim replied. "You may find it hard to stay out of the kitchen!"

"Not a chance, my friend! Not a chance! And remember your promise to me. Not a word about my usual occupation. I'm just going to be your old friend Stephanie to everyone."

"No worries. Your secret is safe with me. There will be no StevieV on board. This is the break you need."

Kim explained that all 105 crew and staff members, as well as all the officers, attended the party when their shifts allowed. The diversity was obvious.

"It's like the United Nations here," Stephanie murmured, eager to learn where everyone was from.

Liam spotted them from across the room and came over to greet them. He and Kim took turns introducing her around, with Liam filling in the details.

"Everything will be cleaned up by ten tonight, so the kitchen and dining room staff can prepare to greet arriving passengers with a brunch buffet tomorrow," he explained. "Dinner tomorrow evening will be their first proper meal on board."

Several other staff joined their conversation, happy to share advice with Stephanie and relating amusing stories of life aboard ship. One topic upon which they all agreed was that she must not miss the first port departure the next day.

"It's quite the experience. One you will never forget," Monica, one of the concierge team, said. "When those sails unfurl for the first time, it's absolutely magical. Everyone gathers on deck and champagne is served."

"And there will be a buffet of tapas and other light

snacks to carry everyone over to dinner," added Jean-Luc, one of the head chefs. "I'm sure Kim has warned you that on a cruise like this, the greatest challenge you will ever have is to resist food."

"Mon Dieu!" his wife, Nicole, a server, interjected. "The best approach is to just give in to temptation and indulge yourself. You can work it all off later."

Stephanie laughed. "I can only imagine——and I've seen photos! That's why our plan is to go for a long hike at every port of call."

Everyone agreed that was a great idea, and several of them offered suggestions of places to go, based on their years of experience.

"Whoa!" Stephanie said, grinning. "I can see I'm going to do some serious note taking." She exchanged phone numbers with some in the group who promised to text her their recommendations.

True to Liam's prediction, the party was over by ten o'clock, and Kim and Stephanie settled into their comfortable beds shortly thereafter. The alarm was set for six.

Chapter 5

Sailing Away

The morning slipped by in a flash as the two friends turned the shelves and countertops of Kim's boutique into attractive displays. All the silver gleamed, the gems glistened, and the rainbow of colors in beaded pieces glowed.

Passengers began to board shortly after eight o'clock and some wandered in with eager questions about the jewelry, even though the shop would not open until after the ship had left the port. Stephanie was impressed.

"I can see how so many people are already interested in your jewelry, Kim," she said. "Are you sure you have a big enough inventory? I'm getting excited before we even begin."

"I've got several bins in storage below decks. Not to worry," Kim assured her. "And just remember, it's one thing to be interested and another to actually make the purchase. You'll see."

When everything was laid out to their satisfaction, they went down to the crew dining room for brunch.

"Even though we are considered staff and are invited to eat in the main dining area, most of the time I prefer to eat down here," Kim explained as they took the stairs down to the fourth level. "It's more fun with everyone coming and going and—bonus—no one will interrupt us to talk about the jewelry. The food is just as good, trust me on that."

The breakfast buffet offered an abundant selection, and a young sous-chef, Carlos, was at one station whipping up custom omelettes. He greeted Kim enthusiastically with a distinctive Spanish accent. "Hey there, welcome back Senorita Keemberly! Did you have a good break in Barcelona? And this must be your friend from Toronto. Bienvenido!"

Kim introduced Stephanie, and Carlos peppered them with questions about what they had seen and done in Barcelona.

"Aha, si, flamenco! Tight pants on handsome men," he said teasingly.

Laughing, Kim said, "Oh yeah. We noticed. But the women were beautiful, and awesome dancers too!"

"So, you liked it too, Senorita Estefania?"

Grinning, Stephanie nodded. "I was smitten—seriously—by the men and the women!"

"Olé!" Carlos exclaimed. "Do you know we have two flamenco dancers on board for entertainment for a few days?"

"No!" both friends exclaimed at the same time. "That's fantastic news!"

"*Si*, they are a couple. I've met them before and they are *fantastico*. They are just on board to perform until we dock in Nice, and they promised to dance for us down here too."

They all agreed to meet for that performance as Carlos put the finishing touches on their omelettes.

He waved them off with a twinkle in his eye and a cheery, "*Hasta leugo*, senoritas! *Mucho gusto*, Estefania!"

"Yes, see you soon, Carlos. Nice to meet you too."

Kim gave Stephanie a sly grin as they sat down to eat. "A handsome, single, Spanish guy and he certainly seemed delighted to meet you."

Stephanie blushed. "Stop it! Yes, he's definitely a charmer What is it about Spanish men? They're all so good looking—. And those accents!—Olé to that too."

"Too bad you aren't interested in meeting anyone."

"Not going to happen. But he seemed like a good guy to hang out with."

Kim nodded knowingly, a twinkle in her eye. Then she announced she was going to have a post-brunch nap before departure.

They parted ways, and Stevie settled in a quiet corner of the deck with an audiobook on her phone. There was only one problem with putting in her earphones—she'd made a playlist that was more suitable for a pity party. She wasn't certain she could ignore it.

And she didn't. Before clicking on the book, she opened her music app and played the song she had listened to countless times since Benny broke up with her.

The searing guitar and soulful tones of Jann Arden's iconic song "Insensitive" filled her head. She never knew when it would make her seriously melancholy and thankfully this time it did not. But she still couldn't quit the song. In a weird way, it even felt comforting. Perhaps she was moving on. Hopefully.

She closed her eyes, and a soft breeze blew over her as the words filled her head. The book could wait. Benny had been insensitive, to say the least. But she would get over him. She had to.

Just after twelve-thirty there was an announcement that the ship would depart in thirty minutes. Everyone was invited to be on deck at that time.

Stevie broke free from her thoughts with a start and dashed to their cabin to freshen up. She and Kim almost collided as she flew through the door. After they stopped laughing, they changed clothes and were ready to go on deck in a matter of minutes.

Passengers were assembling on the various decks around the ship, and waiters were making the rounds with trays of champagne flutes. There was an air of excitement as Captain Keeling announced the ship was departing for their first port of call, Marseille.

Over the sound system the opening notes of Beethoven's emotion-filled Ode to Joy from his Ninth Symphony, floated through the air with all of its glory. Jaws dropped and glasses were raised, and everyone toasted while the white sails slowly unfurled and the ship began to glide out to sea.

Kim wiped tears from her cheeks. "This gets me every time," she whispered.

"It's spectacular," Stephanie whispered, gulping back her emotions.

They stood and watched until all the sails had filled with air.

"Do they always play this music?" Stephanie asked.

"Every time we depart. When we arrive in some ports they play a few different pieces, but all of them are equally touching. Imagine some of Bocelli's songs in Italy —" Kim ended with a sigh.

A nod from Stephanie said it all.

Kim continued, "We have to open soon. Let's find a quiet spot and finish our champagne."

Some people began to settle in deck chairs or lean against the rails to watch the skyline of Barcelona slip away. Others wandered inside to the bars or the casino. The action was getting under way.

Kim and Stephanie leaned over a railing and stared at the endless deep blue stretching before them. The movement of the water as the ship's prow gracefully cut through the waves was mesmerizing. There was something about being on the sea that they both agreed felt peaceful and reassuring.

Stephanie's thoughts turned to the young pregnant widow, Paola, leaving all she had ever known and loved behind. She wondered if her great-grandmother had felt some of that same reassurance on her ship. She hoped so.

She felt a lump rise in her throat. Her entire body suddenly became awash with feelings of sadness mixed with frustration as she considered the situation she had left behind in Toronto.

Bisnonna had never once expressed disappointment

in her. She had always believed in her and filled her with positivity. *Now is not the time to let her down. She always told me to believe in myself and that's what I've got to do. I've got to find a way out of this hole I'm in.*

She rubbed her fingers over the tarot card tattoo and focussed on feeling a connection to Paola's spirit and the joy she always promised. *There are clouds surrounding me right now, Bisnonna—, even at this beautiful moment, but I promise to work on that—*

Kim interrupted her thoughts. "Okay, Stevie-boo. Let's go and make some passengers happy. Bling time!"

CHAPTER 6

MARSEILLE

Stephanie tried to hang back and take her cues from Kim as women crowded the display counter. But it was only a matter of minutes before she was pressed into service. She smiled at one who had asked her a question and tried to sound as knowledgeable as possible about the bracelet the passenger was interested in.

As calm as she always was under pressure in the restaurant kitchen, Stephanie could feel sweat dripping down her back here. She hoped her smile did not betray her nerves, as she carefully placed the bracelet on a velvet tray. Her act seemed to do the trick, because the customer examined the elegant woven silver rope for just a few seconds before declaring that she would buy it.

Everything was tagged with a price and card payment was easy. Stephanie was surprised that the woman didn't haggle about the cost. But after she'd sold a few more items, she realized that none of the customers did. She hadn't believed Kim when she had assured her that the discreetly placed framed notices did their job, but it was true. They did. Written with elegant calligraphy and in French, Italian, Spanish and English, they simply stated: All prices firm. Thank you.

Kim flashed her reassuring glances and the odd wink to let her know she was doing just fine. Sales were brisk. But there were also many who said they would look now and come back at their leisure.

After two hours there was a bit of a break in the action.

"Whew!" Stephanie gave Kim a look of surprise. "I had not expected that crowd."

Kim laughed. "The first day is always like that on this cruise. Everyone seems eager to buy something special to remember the trip and they don't stop to think they have a whole month. I don't get it, but that was my experience on the last cruise and in reports from my employees on earlier cruises. Things should definitely calm down after today and then it is fun because you get to know some of the passengers when they really take their time."

"But where has the crowd suddenly gone?"

"Four o'clock cocktails. And munchies, tapas. Life revolves around food on this cruise, you'll see. We stay open until dinner tonight and, every once in a while, we will have a late-night special event which is always fun!"

Stephanie nodded. "I looked at the schedule in our room. The hours are pretty random at times."

Kim reminded her that due to Customs regulations, the shops had to be closed when the boat was in port. "That's how we get so much time to hike and do what we want."

"I was so excited about coming, I totally forgot that! Cool!"

Stephanie had seen there were four other shops plus theirs: a closet-sized clothing shop that only sold the cruise line t-shirts, hoodies, hats and scarves; a gift shop with candles, serving pieces, ceramics–many with nautical themes; one with toiletries and skincare items; and one offering snacks, soft drinks, and magazines in many languages.

The other shopkeepers had welcomed Kim back during the cocktail party and were introduced to Stephanie. Throughout the afternoon, they all waved their encouragement from time to time in the midst of a constant flow of browsers and buyers. Now it was quiet, they came over to chat.

"It's easier for us to slip away for a few minutes than it is for you with the jewelry," Katie Rose from the clothing shop said. "We can just put a sign on the door. We see our shops from here anyway. How did you manage your first day on the job, Stephanie?"

Stephanie grinned. "Thank goodness Kim is such a pro and so unflappable. Whenever I felt myself at a loss for words, she stepped in seamlessly."

"Ha!" Kim interjected. "Don't let Stephanie fool you. She has the gift of the gab on any subject."

Harvey from the gift shop said, "You two seemed to be putting on quite a show. I've never heard so much laughter before from people spending money!"

⚓

The first port of call was Marseille. Arrival was scheduled for 10:30 the next morning, with the ship cruising at a relaxed speed that offered great comfort to the passengers. A calm sea for the first day and night had eased the transition to sea legs for everyone.

A land excursion, including a tour of the city, was planned for the afternoon, followed by dinner at a classic restaurant that specialized in bouillabaisse.

Liam sat with Kim and Stephanie at breakfast in the officers' dining room. "So, my lovelies, I'm inviting you to put your trust in me and go to a grotty hangout in the oldest part of the port. It's so grungy I wouldn't dare tell our passengers about it. There, I guarantee you will dine on the most delicious bouillabaisse in the world."

Stephanie's eyes sparkled at the suggestion. "How can we refuse? I've never met a bouillabaisse I didn't like, so you are tempting me. And I like grotty and old. Especially when I'm with someone who knows the place."

Kim looked uncertain. "I'll go for the adventure but not for that soup. I can't take all those fisheyes staring at me from the broth!"

"Righty-ho! No fisheyes for you. I have another idea," Liam said. "I'm on duty until three and will meet you around four. One of the great things about Marseille is that we can dock right at a pier for smaller ships. We can hop on a tram that will take us to Vieux Port in less than a half hour, so we'll have time to stop at a local hangout on the way to the bistro. The old port has great character."

"Perfect," Kim said.

Liam was punctual. At four o'clock, he was steering Kim and Stephanie down the gangway and over to a sign that indicated a tram stop. They had to wait only a few minutes before one arrived. Sleek and swift, the tram soon deposited them at the Vieux Port, where they strolled the quay for a while before stopping at a crowded terrace on the water.

"La Bar de la Marine," Liam announced with great flair. "A local gem! Pagnol used it as the setting for his famous film trilogy, *Marius, Fanny*, and *César*. And *Love Actually* had some scenes shot here. If we can get in after dinner, we may catch some great jazz and be entertained by the bartenders at the zinc-topped bar. It's always a blast and so 1930's!"

Kim gushed. "*Love Actually* is one of my all-time favourite movies. I need to check out the inside."

After they were seated, Liam said, "It's time for an *apéro*, as four o'clock is the classic cocktail hour in France. May I suggest an Aperol Spritz?"

Stephanie blanched. How many summer afternoons had she and Benny spent on a terrace in Little Italy sipping those bright orange concoctions? The thought of him was sharp and painful and surprised her. She'd been careful to keep her ex out of her thoughts after her lapse yesterday.

Kim clapped her hands. "Soooo refreshing just to look at them," she gushed as the large bowled wine glasses were placed before them.

"And because they are low in alcohol, we can drink lots of them," Liam added.

They savored their drinks slowly as conversation flowed. The lively atmosphere was catching and Stephanie soon banished thoughts of Benny. She knew it would not be the last time they returned to haunt her.

Liam wanted to hear about the longstanding friendship she and Kim shared, and they soon had him holding his sides as he laughed at their escapades. In turn he regaled them with stories about his family he obviously adored, which included a son who was two years old and a daughter just turning five.

"If it wasn't for video calls, I wouldn't be able to keep doing this job. And I do love the work too."

He explained how his wife, Shelagh, had been the public relations director for the cruise company when he met her and often was able to go along on trips. "That all changed with the arrival of my daughter, of course—and posed some difficult choices. So far, it's all working out, though."

With their thirst quenched, Liam whisked them farther along the quay. They stopped to admire the impressive cathedral of Notre Dame de la Gard overlooking the harbour from high on the hill across the bay.

"It's worth a visit," Liam said, after briefly telling them its history. "But if you still plan to hike tomorrow, you will just have to visit Marseille another time. Kim, you have the bus schedule I gave you?"

"I sure do. Thanks for the directions to the *sentier* too," Kim said. "It looks like the perfect starter path for us."

"And our hiking boots are right by the door, ready to go," Stephanie added.

Liam grinned. "You will love discovering one of Marseilles' famous calanques, and it should not be too crowded in early June——although these days you just never know."

He guided them a little farther along the quay before making a sharp turn into a long alley. After climbing some steep stairs, they walked through a maze of narrow streets, sometimes encountering women in traditional robes and headscarves and men wearing fezzes or skull-caps. Colorful mosaic tiles decorated window surrounds and doorways.

"It feels like we're suddenly visiting a different foreign country. The sounds, the smells——it's another world, very exotic," Kim said, as they continued their walk. It took them past cafés with terraces and tiny shops, sun-baked buildings topped with red-tile roofs, and many pots of bright flowers hanging from peeling shutters.

"You become immersed in the diversity of the city here," Liam said. "You're seeing the Maghreb culture here —people whose roots are in Morocco, Tunisia and Algeria. It's this blend of cultures that makes Marseille so special."

They strolled for a while, stopping to take photos from time to time. Then Liam gestured them into a small passageway, announcing they had arrived at the restau-rant. Stephanie could not see one anywhere, but farther along there was a nondescript doorway. Liam held a beaded curtain aside for the women to go in first. The windowless room was dark and crowded with wooden tables; candlelight glowed. The warm ambiance and tantalizing spice-filled air welcomed them as they were guided to a corner table with a reserved sign. It was the only empty one left.

Liam was greeted like an old friend with *bises* by the staff. He grinned somewhat shyly as he explained he had been coming to the restaurant for years. "You will see why. The food is divine." Steaming cauldrons could be seen being stirred in the open kitchen.

He filled them in on more of the history of the neighbourhood explaining that in most large cities, immigrant communities tended to become established separately in the banlieues or suburbs. "But in Marseille, there is one big community ... this city ... and all cultures assimilate in its heart. No matter where someone originally comes from, they call themselves *Marseillais* first. It's a very special place."

"It's like a small village inside the city. I love this about Europe and it simply is not replicated in the same way in North America," Kim said.

Liam nodded. "Just not possible. These neighbourhoods go back centuries."

"That deep history is one of the reasons I fell in love with life on this side of the Atlantic when I spent my time in Florence and Venice ..." Stephanie's voice trailed off as memories of that time came flooding back.

When Liam asked, "What were you doing there?", she realized she had blurted too much. She wasn't sure what to say, but right then Kim had a coughing fit that gave Stephanie time to come up with a story.

"It was a follow-up to my university business degree. Boring classes but magnificent settings," she said. Then she declared she was going to the ladies' room with Kim, who was still pretending to have something caught in her throat.

"Whew! That was close I've got to be more careful about what I say," Stephanie said as soon as they were out of his hearing. "Thanks for the coughing spasm. Well done."

"Always there for the save," Kim laughed.

When they returned to the table, a selection of appetizers and warm flatbread was waiting. They had agreed at the bar that they would forego bouillabaisse that evening, as it was readily available, and that Liam would take them somewhere special for a taste of a different cuisine. He had made a quick phone call.

Course after course arrived at the table, each more delicious than the last. An aromatic lamb tajine was served in such colorful ceramic pottery that Stephanie and Kim instantly enquired about purchasing one. Liam arranged for the pots to be delivered to the ship the next morning.

"This is all home cooking using recipes passed down through generations," Liam explained, as they scooped up the meat, vegetables and buttered saffron rice with Moroccan flatbread. "This tajine is the *pièce de résistance*."

They all agreed wholeheartedly.

⚓

After finishing the meal with several cups of steaming mint tea, the threesome wandered back to La Bar de la Marine. They opted to sit outside, agreeing that the crammed interior was still an uncomfortable choice because of Covid, even if the worst of it was over. Music carried out the bar's open doors and windows—a fusion of jazz, blues and belly dancing rhythms. They could hear voices and laughter between the notes, and see the crowd inside swaying. The feeling of being immersed in the multiethnic swirl of Marseille made it a most memorable evening.

A tram was already waiting at the stop to take them back to the port, and Liam blushed at the profuse thanks Stephanie and Kim gave him on the short trip. "Not at all. The pleasure was mine," he insisted.

Back in their cabin, the two friends lay in bed reliving the evening. Stephanie confessed how thoughts of Benny had popped into her head when the aperol spritzes were ordered. "That was *our* drink. For a few short moments, I truly missed him. It's not that easy to accept we aren't together anymore."

"I hear you," Kim replied. "You've shared a lot of years as a couple, and made a lot of memories. It hurts to know that is over, and the pain isn't going to simply go away. Some days you have to let those sad thoughts in and grieve the loss."

Stevie felt tears well and buried her face in her pillow. She had been keeping those emotions locked up for weeks and knew it was time to let them out. Before long she was doing something she hadn't done since her beloved Paola passed. She was sobbing uncontrollably.

Kim sat beside her on the bed and rubbed her back. "Real tears, my friend. It's about time."

"I—I—need to s-s-s-stop ..." Stephanie stammered. "I don't do tears!"

"Well, you do now," Kim said. "This is the best thing for you, Stevie. Let it out. It won't be the last time either —, speaking from experience. You've certainly helped me more than once. Grieving——and that's what you are doing——is an ongoing process. It takes time."

Between rounds of weeping, Stephanie rambled, questioning whether she had been working too hard and not paying Benny enough attention.

Kim assured her that was not the case. "You were a team. I always admired that. He was good to you and you to him——bringing food home, exercising together. You both kept your condo sparkling. You helped him with some of his courses. He helped you with social media for the bistro. Don't beat yourself up for something that isn't true."

"Then why did he leave me?" Stephanie wailed. "Why? After all those years?"

Kim spoke softly. "Who knows? But the Covid lockdown affected many of us in strange ways. Perhaps when you get back to Toronto the two of you can have a talk. He owes you the truth."

"Maybe——or maybe I will be over this by the time I get back and I won't want to talk to him," Stephanie said. She sat up and blew her nose.

"I have a theory," Kim said softly. "I'm still working on it, and I don't want to lay it all on you now. But consider this——maybe your breakup didn't just happen now. We agreed you were a team—but I think at some point you stopped being lovers. I don't mean this to be hurtful but here's my take: you've been without a warm, passionate relationship for some time, and Benny leaving was the final slam of the door."

Stephanie looked at her for a long moment. She nodded slowly. Her voice was low and halting when she spoke. "Friends with benefits, as they say. His leaving was a shock but in fact you are right. It's been ages since we behaved like lovers."

They sat without talking for a while as Stephanie emptied the box of tissues.

After a few false starts, she declared she was done with the tears. "Thanks for the support. You always know what to do."

"Ha!" Kim snorted. "Not always. But I think I'm in a pretty good place right now."

"That's kind of a weird thing to say after two years of lockdown." Stephanie said. "Do you really think the Covid years impacted you in a positive way? I was so flipping busy cooking, I don't think I ever asked you. Did you change anything in your life?"

Kim nodded. She stood up and crossed to the window. "For sure. You know how focused I was on meeting a new man of my dreams before the pandemic hit. Sheesh, some days it seemed I had a revolving door, with all the dates I accepted. But lockdown proved to me that I could be happy on my own. Now that dreamboat can stay out there. If I never meet him, I couldn't care less."

She motioned for Stephanie to join her at the window. "Come and look at these amazing stars."

Stephanie was quiet for a few moments. Then she slipped out of bed and stood by Kim. There was no moon that night, so the sky over the sea seemed filled with stars. "Wow, that is a spectacular show! How peaceful and calming is that?"

"Exactly," Kim said. "Now don't you feel better for getting those tears out?"

"I can't believe I wept so much—but I do feel better. Between forgetting about being dumped and weaning myself from cooking for another month, I've still got a lot of change to work on. To think I almost blew the cooking part tonight too! Thanks again for coughing."

Kim chuckled. "I wondered what the heck you were going to say. But you handled it well."

Stephanie yawned sleepily, and they both returned to their beds. "Deception was never one of my skills," she sighed. "I'll have to think more before I open my mouth. On the other hand, we sure had a great time tonight. I wonder if every port is going to deliver such wonderful experiences. Liam is the best guide."

"Time will tell, Steviebean! Time will tell," Kim murmured, drifting off. "I can't wait for tomorrow."

CHAPTER 7

HIKING THE CALANQUES

They were on the pier by 7:30 the next morning, and soon found the stop for the bus that would take them to their trailhead in the Parc national des Calanques.

For forty-five minutes, before Marseille awakened, they enjoyed the quiet views of the normally bustling city. Their surroundings changed dramatically as the bus left the city and climbed into the surrounding rugged hills. The route bordered the sea now and looking down they could see steep limestone cliffs plunging into the translucent turquoise waters.

Soon the bus came to a stop, and the friendly driver pointed out the beginning of the trail not far away. They could see a few other hikers already setting out, and the map Liam had given Kim clearly indicated where they were to go.

The winding path of sand and gravel they took was bordered by the Mediterranean *garrigue*. Dense, scrubby vegetation, it filled the air with the mingled scents of rosemary, lavender, sage and thyme.

"Mmm. Breathe that in," Kim instructed, opening her arms wide and lifting her head to the sky. She inhaled loudly and then said softly, but pointedly, "It's definitely the kind of perfumed air that helps heal a broken heart."

"Amazing! Instant aromatherapy." Stephanie copied her and threw her arms up. "I didn't miss that comment. I'm trying. Honest!"

"I know you are," Kim murmured as she slipped her arm around Stevie's shoulders.

They stood still for a few moments, eyes closed, breathing in the goodness in the air. When they started off, they moved slowly and let their heads fill with the fragrances.

Before long they stopped at a viewpoint offering a panoramic vista of a long fjord-like bay, one of the many *calanques* that pierced the limestone cliffs along this stretch of the coast. The sun reflected dazzlingly off the water, which varied from being crystalline to the deepest azure.

"This is like the best high I could imagine, except when I'm breathing in cooking aromas, of course, and that doesn't count now." Stephanie said. She swept her hand around at the view. "The combination of the view and the smells here is mind blowing!"

Kim pulled out her phone and tapped its screen. "The park's website states that most of the trails around les calanques are closed in the summer due to the risk of fires," she said. "We're lucky to have a chance to hike this one now."

There were two options. One was to hike all the way around to the other side of the calanque on the clifftop and the other was to take a steep, winding path down to sea level. They opted for the second choice.

As they neared the bottom of the trail they could see there was not much in the way of sandy beach. The few people already there were sitting and sunbathing on flat areas of the rocks. It was obvious that on hot summer days there would be a lot of jumping into the water. The setting called for it. They had not planned to swim, knowing the water would still be quite cold, although a few hardy souls were ignoring that.

They found their own flat rock to sit upon and basked in the warm sunshine for a while enjoying the beauty of the rugged nature surrounding them. Then they slipped off their boots and rolled up their pants to dangle their feet in the refreshing sea.

After a while, Stephanie continued her lament about Benny. This time she kept her tears in check.

"I did enough crying last night to last me for a while. But you know, it was one thing for Ben to drop the bomb that he was leaving me. And quite another to say it was because he and Guido were in love with each other. Now I have all sorts of questions that I wish I had asked him at the time. I was just in too much shock to even think straight."

"No kidding, I can't even imagine," Kim said, her words full of sympathy. "You were all such good friends. I even thought about taking a run at Guido once when we were all together. He's the whole package—great body, looks, personality." She shook her head in disbelief and tossed a few pebbles into the water, watching as the ripples faded away.

They mused over several scenarios about Guido and Ben hooking up, before deciding they had spent enough time on the subject for now. "To be continued," Stephanie promised.

Hiking back to the top of the cliff was not quite so easy as the trail was slippery with loose gravel in some of the steeper parts.

At the top, they chose a route that would take them two hours to reach the road again.

"I think that will be long enough for our first hike," Kim said. "Your boots look like slippers but, as you noticed, mine are brand new. I'll have to break them in slowly."

Stephanie nodded. "My boots have racked up a ton of kilometres. They're incredibly comfy."

The trail took them longer than two hours as they repeatedly stopped to take in a spectacular view of a long vista stretching out to sea. They couldn't get enough of the stunning scenery and of the richly scented garrigue. When they got back to the road, they were happy to see a conveniently located café offering a limited menu of fresh fish dishes had just opened. Lunch was on!

Chapter 8

Meeting Martha

Kim and Stephanie were on duty behind the jewelry counter by apéros. There had been time for a shower and a quick nap, and they were both eager to get back to work. The ship was not as busy as it had been the previous evening because today many passengers were taking an afternoon city tour, which would culminate with dinner at a Michelin star restaurant.

Ryley, the charismatic bartender across the way sent over a waitress with a glass of local rosé for each of them.

A steady stream of passengers who had chosen to stay on board wandered by, mainly women, relaxed and friendly and holding their own glass of wine. Several stopped by the shop to browse and try on jewelry. The atmosphere was light and casual and many of the customers were keen to chat. Knowing they were unable to buy while in port, they had pieces put on hold.

Enjoying the party atmosphere, Stephanie was aware of the different languages and accents she heard amongst the women. Liam had mentioned there were twelve different countries represented on the passenger list.

Stephanie was reminded of her early years when she waited tables at Cara Mia and how much fun it had been to interact with customers. For many years since then, she had been in the kitchen cooking and creating, with little time to chat to diners. She revelled in the socializing now.

Kim sidled up to her at one point and said, under her breath, "There's nothing like looking at jewelry to get women interacting. So much fun!"

She was surprised to learn that quite a number of the passengers had not signed up for the gourmet dining offered on the cruise. Many said they preferred to explore the ports of call on their own and find interesting local bars and restaurants.

A woman with stunning white hair styled in a fashionable bob, walked over and raised her glass. "A toast to two more Canadians on the ship! Ryley just told me I have company."

Appearing to be in her sixties, she had a youthful sparkle in her eyes and her grin lit up the space around her. "Hi there, I'm Martha Francescatto. So pleased to meet you both."

Stephanie and Kim raised their glasses in return and then there were fist bumps all around.

"Interesting how we are all still a bit leery of the old-fashioned handshake," Martha said. "I guess we have a way to go to get back to our old habits——if we ever do." Stevie and Kim nodded in agreement.

"Where are you from, Martha?" Kim asked.

"I lived in the heart of Toronto for most of my life. I worked at the University of Toronto, but I retired seven years ago. When Covid hit I moved to Vancouver to be near my grandkids. Now I spend my time hiking the mountains of beautiful British Columbia. How about you?"

Kim and Stephanie told her where they were from, and when Martha heard Little Italy mentioned, her eyes lit up. "Ah, I lived in the Kensington Market area and spent most of my life eating in Little Italy. Such a lively neighbourhood, with some of the most eclectic restaurants in the city."

As she said that, Martha gave Stephanie a curious look——almost of recognition.

Stevie blinked rapidly then noticed another woman at the counter was trying to catch her attention about a bracelet. Feeling a sliver of relief at being distracted, she apologized to Martha, saying, "So nice to meet you. Let's talk again soon."

Martha replied, "Absolutely! I'm off to the spa, but I'll be back to do some serious retail therapy here in the coming days. You can bet on that." She left them with a cheery wave.

CHAPTER 9

NICE, CÔTE D'AZUR

The next morning, the gentle movement of the boat rocked Stephanie out of a deep sleep. They were on the move.

She opened her eyes to see Kim sitting at the window, her morning chai tea on the table next to her. But Stevie's keen sense of smell also detected the heady scent of strong espresso.

"You are the best roomie ever! It's such a treat to have my morning shot of joe waiting for me," Stephanie murmured, stretching to reach the tiny cup Kim was handing her.

"Thank goodness for these fantastic espresso machines. Pop in a pod and—badda bing, badda boom—liquid gold. I wish I liked it. I love the smell but, as you know, I can't handle the taste."

Laughing, Stephanie teased her about the number of times she had tried to convert Kim to espresso through the years.

"You know I never react to caffeine in any form. All

my life I've felt like I've been missing out on the great caffeine boost," Kim complained.

"And you know what I keep telling you——it's about the crema too. That combination of the smooth froth floating on top with the sharp coffee below is what delivers the punch. It's so rich. So bold. *Madonna! Fantastica!*"

"Well, I can tell you'll be ready to face the world once you finish that. Come and sit by the window and watch the south coast of France pass by. We are on our way to Nice, where most cruise ships can't dock as the harbour is too small. But we're special, and we will be right in the thick of the action."

This would be a full day at sea, with the ship travelling slowly to allow the passengers to enjoy the beauty of the coast.

The view was straight out of the best travel video. A sliver of bright turquoise sea separated the ship from a stunning landscape dotted with villages in subdued earth tones, simple farmhouses baking under the bright sun and sprawling villas set amid lush gardens. Stevie gasped at the beauty, and Kim turned on the iPad found in each cabin and tapped the link to the ship's article on the coastline. Not only did it describe what they were seeing, but also gave a brief history of the towns they would be passing.

"Let's bring breakfast back here and listen while we eat," Kim suggested. "I'll go get it. Remember, I saw all of this on the last trip. I want you to enjoy it."

After breakfast, it was time to open the shop. With the iPad set up on a counter, they did not miss a thing and customers watched it with them. Much of the view they could see through the window across from the shop.

"We won't be very busy today as everyone will be doing the same as us, watching this glorious scenery go by," Kim said.

The ship moved slowly toward Cassis allowing a close-up view of the many dramatic cliff-lined calanques along the way.

"I'm so glad we got to experience at least one of those beautiful spots. I'd be up for coming back to hike around all of them. How stunning would that be?" Stephanie said.

Kim gave her a thumbs up. "Add it to the list—— which is going to stretch for a mile by the time this cruise is finished. Trust me on that."

The ship passed the picturesque harbors of La Ciotat, Bandol, and Sanary-sur-Mer as well as the large naval base at Toulon, so vital to the victory of World War II.

"I'm really glad they've included these historical details," Stephanie said. "What a fantastic way to learn about these places as we see them."

After they passed the urban sprawl of Toulon, they sailed faster along a stretch of coast with sandy beaches and what were once fishing villages but were now mostly holiday towns. Beyond them, gentle hills dotted by villages folded up from the sea.

After passing flotillas of luxury yachts around St. Tropez, the landscape changed dramatically. Le massif d'Estérel's rugged hills of red volcanic rock dominated the coast until Cannes came into view.

The ship slowed again to allow the full pleasure of viewing the stunning landscape of the Côte d'Azur all the way to Nice.

The towns on this coast were protected by rolling hills, which guaranteed the temperate climate. Behind the hills, they could see the peaks of the majestic Alps. Stephanie declared it was a sight to behold.

"I will never call it the French Riviera again," she said. "La Côte d'Azur has such a classy ring to it and it's even more beautiful than I imagined. Look at those stunning villas along the Cap d'Antibes and just read this history!"

Kim patted her on the shoulder. "We are going to hike the sentier that goes all around there. You'll get to see all that close up!"

"Awesome!" Stephanie said. "I can't wait!"

Soon, the *Dream Maker* approached the harbour in Nice, where a crowd had gathered at the entrance to watch its graceful arrival in full sail.

"I'm falling in love all over again," Stephanie sighed, as Liam led them through the harbour that evening at the start of another of his walking tours. They hadn't got far when Katherine, the staff captain rushed up to join them.

"I can't let Liam be your sole tour guide here," she said. "I love Nice and may someday return to live here. I want to show you my favorite places too."

Liam made an overly grudging face and muttered his agreement to have her join them, but then put his arm around her shoulders and gave her an affectionate squeeze. "Who knows? You might even show me something I don't know!"

They began at a noisy quayside restaurant with delicious plates of moules-frites (mussels and fries) washed down with cold beer.

The port and old town of Nice proved to be an easy and beautiful area to stroll. Surprising Art Deco architecture, built after World War I, somehow blended with the city's colorful Belle Époque palaces and villas, Baroque churches and centuries-old tenement buildings in a wonderfully eclectic way.

They turned into the warren of twisting narrow streets of the oldest part of vieux Nice, with its 16th century terra cotta buildings. For a time they were swept back in history, imagining how life must have been there. Passing through the vibrant Place Rosetti, Katherine pointed out the long line waiting for ice cream at the family-run Fenocchio ice cream parlour.

"Ninety flavors!" Liam exclaimed. "And I swear I've tried most of them! Ice cream is kind of a rite of passage on the Riviera."

When they suddenly arrived out onto the wide street of Cours Saleya, the atmosphere changed. They were in the midst of a party scene, filled with music and lively conversation. One restaurant terrace after another filled the street, which, Liam told them, the daily market occupied each morning. Walking through an arched opening, they found themselves on the famed Promenade des Anglais.

"Without question, it is one of the most beautiful

main drags in the world!" Liam exclaimed. "How can you beat this? The Prom runs along the sea for about seven kilometres, and it's wide enough for strolling, biking, running, rollerblading, you name it."

"Or simply sitting on one of its famous blue chairs and enjoying the Med at any time, night or day," Katherine added. "There are private beaches here, but they are interspersed with public ones and have marvellous bars and restaurants."

After a long walk on the Promenade, they decided a beach bar would be the perfect place to watch the sunset and end their evening out.

CHAPTER 10

ÈZE

The next morning before breakfast, Kim read aloud the itinerary for the afternoon. "The hike we have planned is a short one. Liam says we can fit it in, no problem. I would like to work on some beading this morning because I noticed a lot of pieces put on hold yesterday. And a group of American women asked if they could stop by this morning to choose something to put away. I will make a private showing for them."

Stephanie knew she could be of no help there. "Excellent! I'm going to sit on the deck with my book after I spend some time sending emails home. Everyone is asking how I'm doing and it's time I gave them an update."

"Okay," Kim said. "Check at the shop with me around 11:30."

Stephanie rubbed her hands in glee. "I can't wait! Then we will need to head out to the bus stop *tout de suite*, as they say. See how bilingual I am once I get to France?"

Kim snorted.

The six women from New York who were travelling together to celebrate their sixtieth birthdays spent some time choosing one piece of jewelry. They planned to each purchase an identical item to commemorate the occasion. The decision was not easy, and it took them some time, but a stunning beaded necklace in varying shades of blue and turquoise was the winner.

"It's the exact colors of the Med," they exclaimed. "How perfect is that?"

Stephanie arrived back at the shop at 11:30 just as Kim had safely set aside the women's treasures. "I'm so glad I made more than one of that necklace. I have to admit I loved the design so much I made those six."

"And I'm sure they were thrilled to know that theirs are the only six that exist." Stephanie replied.

At the same time, Martha passed by, dressed for hiking. She stopped to say hello and Kim asked where she was headed.

"I'm taking the train to Èze-sur-Mer—just two stops —and then I'm hiking up to Èze Village and back down again. It's the trail that Frederich Nietzsche used to walk —every day apparently. I hike it each time I'm here and try to absorb some of his karma as I do. The good part, not the troubled part!" She ended with a loud guffaw.

"We're going to Èze too," Kim said. "The Èze on top of the hill. And then we're going to hike down the Nietzsche Trail. What a coincidence." Kim said.

"Well, hell," Martha replied. "Why don't we meet at the top and hike down together. There's a great place we can stop for a beer on the beach when we are done."

After lunch, each carrying a small backpack, Kim and Stephanie walked down the gangway and along the quay to the street where a sleek tram was passing by. They spotted the #82 bus coming along and broke into a run.

After paying their fare, they chose the best seats for a view of the stunning scenery while the bus wound along the low road of the bass corniche to the picturesque town of Villefranche-sur-Mer. Between narrow streets and multi-colored ancient buildings, they glimpsed steep flights of stairs leading to the bright blue sea.

"We're coming back here for dinner, right?" Stephanie asked. "I've got to explore those streets."

"Right. After we have a beer with Martha on the beach in Èze-sur-Mer. On our way back to Nice, we'll have a wander here and eat at a great café on the harbour. Now get ready to enjoy the hair-raising but spectacular ride up to Èze Village." Kim said.

Just past Villefranche the bus made a left turn and zig-zagged its way up a steep, winding road Stevie would never have believed anyone could drive, let alone a bus. Her vertigo kicked into high gear, but the bus made it without falling over.

As they wandered through the eleventh-century village, Stephanie was at a loss for words. The steep, narrow passages made of uneven stones and steps led to an exotic garden filled with cacti and succulents planted uphill to a castle ruin. From there, they could see as far as the bay of St. Tropez to the west and the coast of Italy to the east.

"This view is mind blowing," Stephanie sputtered. "What an awesome panorama! My year at cooking school in Italy didn't take me to views like this!"

She took out her phone and shot picture after picture.

Kim grinned as though she had been keeping it all a secret. "It's my favorite place for photos on the Riviera. How can you beat this view?"

On their walk through the village back to the arched entry they got lost a few times in the maze of passageways. They laughed each time they realized they had gone in a circle.

"It's so charming here, we could get lost for hours and I wouldn't mind," Stephanie said. "All of this stone —everything breathes history and is so intriguing— simply beautiful."

"And with all this jasmine in bloom, I think I'm getting a little light-headed from the sweet fragrance. I can't stop breathing it in." Kim took another deep breath. "But I think if we turn here, we will be on the way out to the road."

As they passed under the archway of the tower where they had first entered the village, they saw Martha sitting on the stone wall, waving to them just as they had arranged.

"Did you love enchanting Èze?" Martha asked, her eyes glistening.

She looked a bit sweaty but still energetic, Stevie thought, marvelling at her enthusiasm.

They nodded, and Martha continued. "If I only have time to visit one place when I am in this part of France, this is where I come. This captivating village, so alive with history, makes walking up to it well worthwhile, and that stunning view always rejuvenates my spirit. I wouldn't miss it!"

"How many times have you been here?" Kim asked.

"Well my dear, I go waaaaay back. My first visit was in 1962, long before it became really popular with tourists. That's when its magic was truly amazing. But I didn't discover the hiking trail until much later as it had become overgrown. I guess I've been up and down twenty or so times throughout my life. And I've loved it every time—except for the crowds up here in more recent years. But it actually doesn't seem too bad today."

"Nope! I guess we got lucky. We must be in between tour groups," Kim said. "Do you want to have a drink or something to eat before we head down?"

"I'm okay if you are. I packed a lunch and stopped on the way up." Martha said. "Then I had a drink at the little café just before the garden entrance. Thought I might see you."

Stephanie laughed and explained that was probably while they were busy getting lost.

"Well, if we are all ready, let's hit the trail," Kim said. And they set off.

The hike was a little more strenuous than the one they had done on the clifftops at the calanque, but more sheltered. For most of the time, they were walking through wooded areas that suddenly opened up to a breathtaking view. With a few stops to hydrate, they were at the bottom in just over two hours.

Martha led the way across the road and the railroad

tracks to a beach bar. They were now in the village of Èze-sur-Mer. After ordering, they all untied their boots, stripped off their socks and waded into the refreshing sea.

"Wearing a bathing suit might have been a good idea," Stephanie said. "I could dive right in, I'm so hot!"

"Well, this is the Riviera my dear," Martha said, with a straightforward look at both of them. "No bathing costume required. In my younger years I had no problem stripping off completely but now I wear co-ordinated undies."

With that she undid her shirt and shorts, dropped them back on the pebbled beach and dove under the water with a flash of hot pink!

Stephanie's mouth gaped.

Kim laughed and gave Martha a thumbs up when she surfaced. "Obviously we have a lot to learn from you."

Martha declined their invitation to join them for dinner, saying she had plans. Stephanie and Kim made their way back to the train and got off in Villefranche-sur-Mer. Instead of heading straight to a bistro, they spent a few minutes taking photos on the beach that was a short walk away.

"How lovely is this?" Stephanie whispered, as much to herself as Kim.

The shore of the harbour was dotted with colorful umbrellas and tables that furnished the bistro terraces. Boats of all sizes bobbed on the gentle waves, and paddle boarders wove their way around them. The picturesque beach, backed by a long stone wall covered in magenta bougainvillea, was still busy with swimmers.

The timeworn, multi-colored buildings of the old

town appeared to rise out of the sea. Stevie was so taken by a few glimpses up its picturesque streets, she declared she simply had to see it. They headed down a passageway lined with both stone buildings and ones with colorfully painted stucco, and Stevie sensed the centuries-long history that lived on here. She found it impossible not to stop every few paces to take a photo as they wandered along.

"Note to self," Stephanie said. "I need to come back when that Cocteau chapel is open. I can see why he spent so much time here."

Kim was starting to droop from all their walking, so they made their way back to one of the bistros at the water's edge, and both of them ordered a salade Nicoise. The salads arrived topped by a lightly seared tuna steak of exactly the right size. They agreed that it was delicious and just what they needed after all the exercise they had that day.

"Liam was right again. It's the best Nicoise I've ever had," Kim exclaimed with a satisfied grin. Stephanie raised her glass of rosé in agreement.

Chapter 11

Antibes

"I'm soooo excited about today's plan," Stephanie repeated as she danced around the tiny cabin. "After listening to Martha talk about Antibes on our hike yesterday, I can't wait to see the town and I'm sure the sentier there will be stunning."

Kim agreed as she brushed her long hair and pulled it into a knot on top of her head. "It's cool that she has spent so much time in this part of France."

"She's putting ideas in my head that I hadn't considered since I was a dreamer in high school." Stephanie said. "I think I want to be like her when I grow up."

Kim checked the time. "Jean-Luc will be waiting at the gangway in ten minutes, so let's get going. He said he has planned something special for us this morning before we go hiking."

Most of the passengers were disembarking when they arrived, and the level of excitement was high. They were going on a full day tour along the coast and up into the hills before dining at a Michelin-star restaurant in Antibes.

As they watched the crowd disembark, Kim said, "It's so cool that Martha is staying on board. Did you hear her tell me that she loves to have the ship to herself when everyone is touring places she's already been more than once?"

"Awesome," Stevie replied. "She knows what she's doing."

Once the passengers had left, Jean-Luc appeared. "*On y va, mes amies!* I've got an Uber booked so you can enjoy the view all the way to Antibes. The market is just opening now and that's our first stop."

Jean-Luc treated them to a running commentary as the car hugged the sparkling turquoise sea all the way to Antibes, along the Bord de Mer. Stephanie couldn't help interrupting him as they drove into the town.

"This view! This sea! And look at this—you just pull over, park and you're at the beach with food trucks, fishing, whatever you want," Stephanie exclaimed.

Jean-Luc patted her on the cheek. "You sound enamored with all of this."

Kim laughed. "Jean-Luc, she's been falling in love repeatedly ever since she saw flamenco in Barcelona. She's out of control!"

"Oh, mon Dieu! Monique is the same. I love taking her to see flamenco because—well, you know ..." He actually blushed as he spoke. Everyone laughed, even the Uber driver.

"So first we are going to the daily Provençal market," he continued. "I have a cheese order to leave with

Philippe, the best fromager on the Côte d'Azur. We always stock up while we are in port in Nice and he will have it delivered to the ship this afternoon. Although we buy local cheeses wherever we stop during the cruise, we always make sure we have a fine selection of French cheese for the entire month. There's nothing better."

"Wouldn't it be easier to do that online?" Stephanie asked.

"*Bien sûr*," he agreed. "But I never miss visiting this town—it's one of my favourites. You will see why. And Philippe has become a good friend, as well as being the best fromager I know."

"That's an impressive recommendation," Stephanie said.

"I'm not exaggerating—and," he added with a sly grin, "there's no way to taste a great cheese online!"

Then Jean-Luc pointed to the ancient fort that overlooked the old town and, beyond it, to the harbour filled with some of the grandest mega yachts to be found anywhere.

"Jaw-dropping—all of it ..." Stephanie murmured.

The Uber driver dropped them at an archway in the ramparts of the old town, which Jean-Luc said were originally built in the 1500s. The archway entrance gave onto what was becoming a familiar maze of narrow, cobblestone streets, this one as delightful as the ones Stephanie had already seen, and they soon arrived at the daily Provençal market.

It was a hive of activity, with shoppers crowding around stalls and filling their traditional woven wicker baskets or modern rolling carts. From one end of the building to the other, vendors were calling out, encouraging customers to sample their wares. Fresh vegetables, fruit, greens, spices, flowers, filled aged wicker display baskets in the most eye-catching way. Even the butchers, fromagers, and fish mongers had found ways to beautifully display their wares.

"One thing you must never be," Jean-Luc told them, "is in a hurry. You need to look, smell, savor. It's a total experience."

Stephanie had to bite her lip not to mention she'd shopped at markets all her life. Of course, the markets in every country had their own character and she loved that aspect. Shopping in Kensington Market almost daily with Bisnonna Paola was one of her favourite activities as a child. Everyone there knew her name from the time she was a toddler, so it truly felt like they were all family. And market shopping had been a major part of her cooking school in Florence.

But there was no denying the cheese displays in France were the best. And Jean-Luc was right, markets were to be savored. She couldn't resist stopping at many of the stalls before they arrived at the long glass-fronted counter of Fromagerie Philippe DuFour.

Jean-Luc insisted they join the end of the long lineup, which gave them plenty of time to admire the artful displays of cheese of every kind. Once they were inside, Stephanie saw a handsome, middle-aged man speaking with a customer at the head of the queue. His eyes lit up when he spied Jean-Luc, and he asked someone previously hidden behind the counter to take his place.

Philippe rushed over and the men greeted each other with enthusiastic bises. Then Jean-Luc introduced him to Kim and Stephanie.

"These are two Canadians working on our cruise. They are going to hike the *sentier*, around the Cap d'Antibes here today and I wanted them to see the market first," Jean-Luc explained.

"Ah, bon! My wife is also Canadian," Philippe said. "Where exactly are you from?"

When they said Toronto, Philippe broke into a wide grin. "And so is my wife!"

He looked across the market and gestured to a café where an attractive woman with shoulder length blonde hair was pouring a cup of tea from a pot. At the same table was a woman with wild, purple hued hair. They were both laughing uproariously.

After a comment to his colleague, Philippe extended an arm to Kim and Stephanie. Then he led them to the café, with Jean-Luc following.

"Minou, I've brought you some Toronto friends. From Jean-Luc's ship."

Jean-Luc introduced Philippe's wife as Kat, who in turn introduced her friend, Bernadette. Philippe said he had to go back to the cheese stand and Jean-Luc went with him. Kat and Bernadette invited Stephanie and Kim to join them and a waiter promptly arrived to take orders. Stephanie and Kim felt immediately welcomed.

"It's always a pleasure to meet Canadians here," Kat said. "Tell me where you live in the city. I haven't been back in a few years, I must admit. But I loved Toronto while I lived there."

Stephanie found Kat easy to talk to, and Bernadette joined in the conversation enthusiastically, saying she had been to Toronto once after she visited family in Montreal. Bernadette also insisted on telling a short version of how Kat came to be living in Antibes. Stephanie and Kim were enchanted, and Kat admitted she was used to her friend telling the story and feeling partially responsible for her falling in love with Philippe.

Before long they all felt like friends. Kim and Stephanie enjoyed Kat's story of her first home exchange to Provence and how she met Philippe. They plied her with questions about living in Antibes, and Bernadette kept them laughing with her side comments.

"And what are you doing on this visit to our beautiful Antibes?" Kat asked. "How nice that you have the entire day off to spend here"

"We are so glad Jean-Luc brought us through the charming streets of the old town before coming to the market. What a special place it is." Stephanie said.

Kim nodded and added, "You may have guessed from our attire," Kim said. "We want to hike the *sentier littoral*. We've got all the information here. The trail seems to go around the whole of the Cap d'Antibes and end at Juan les Pins."

They all agreed it was a perfect day for this hike, and Bernadette gave them her business card, explaining she was a taxi driver.

"She's the best on the Riviera!" Kat said, and they were happy to know she could take them back to the ship when they finished. That was a detail they had not considered and were shocked when Bernadette advised them how difficult it was to find a taxi or Uber.

"Another victim of the pandemic. We are under-staffed everywhere," Kat said.

Philippe and Jean-Luc joined them again, and Philippe handed Kim a small paper bag. "Here's something to make your day even more perfect."

The others laughed, explaining that Philippe was known for always being quick with gifts of delicious cheese. "That's how he won my heart," Kat said with a smile. "He brought me cheese instead of flowers and I was smitten!"

Philippe slipped his arm around Kat's shoulder, giving it a gentle squeeze. They gazed at each other with a look that made it very clear they were still very much in love.

Stephanie felt a small wrench to her heart and thought about Kim's words. Maybe what she did need was to feel loved again.

"Come back to Antibes," Kat invited. "Philippe and I have a B and B just minutes from here on the Cap and we would love to have you stay. We've had a few guests from Toronto and that's always so special."

"In fact, you can see it from the *sentier*," Bernadette added and drew a quick map on a napkin. "Be sure to look up just as you reach this point." She marked a big x and passed it to them. "You can't miss it."

"And Bernadette is our unofficial official driver who will collect you from wherever you are," Philippe said.

Kim and Stephanie both said how much they would love to do just that. "You never know! We'll be a bit footloose and fancy free for a while when the cruise is over," Kim said.

Jean-Luc insisted on walking them to the beginning of the trail, just a short way past the beach near the market. He waved them off after extracting promises they would text from time to time to let him know they were fine.

"At least we know you will have an entertaining ride back to the ship with Bernadette," he said with a chuckle. "À tout à l'heure!"

CHAPTER 12

CAP D'ANTIBES

Using the GPS on her phone, Kim led the way, dodging traffic along the busy road until they reached the Plage de la Garoupe. Beach restaurants were being set up for lunch service and many of the lounge chairs on the sand were already occupied.

"That looks so inviting," Kim said. "Maybe we should strip to our bathing suits and join the beach crowd."

Stephanie laughed. She agreed it was tempting but said, "Nope, we're sticking to our plan."

Kim gave them both a good spritz from her spray can of water and they set off, cooled for the moment.

Kat and Bernadette had cautioned them not to be dismayed by the bilingual sign at the beginning of the path that said in English "Warning. Very dangerous walk while squall."

"It's a beautiful, calm day so there is nothing to worry about," Kat had said. "It's only when the winds are high that the trail truly should be avoided."

The narrow rocky path hugged the coast, sometimes well above and sometimes at the same level as the multicolored Mediterranean, with steep sets of stairs to climb up and the limestone cliffs that plunged into the sea. On the first part of their hike, whenever they looked behind them there was a breathtaking view across to the ancient towers of the old town with the rugged peaks of the Alps in the background. From time to time, they caught a glimpse through flowering shrubs of sumptuous villas offering hints of a luxurious life on the Cap d'Antibes.

"*Oh là là!*" Stevie exclaimed. "Talk about lifestyles of the rich and famous. *Excusez-moi!*"

"Just imagine how life was here between the two world wars, which was when the Americans discovered the Riviera. It seems all of the big names in the arts were in Paris and the south of France: Hemingway, Fitzgerald, Stein, Picasso, Matisse to name just a few," Kim said.

"I read a great biography of that rich American couple, the Murphys, who befriended F. Scott Fitzgerald and the other writers and painters. They introduced Fitzgerald to jazz and he really got into promoting that music here. He rented a private villa that is now a swanky hotel, I think it's called Belles Rives. He would lock the doors so the musicians couldn't leave. They would party until sunrise."

Kim waved her hands in the air and did a little shimmy. "It's delightful. It's delicious. It's de-lovely" she sang.

"The Jazz Age, the Roaring Twenties, Cole Porter and all those songs—what a time it must have been!" Stevie said.

"Do do that voodoo that you do so well," Kim sang again, twirling around, then pointed at Stevie to come up with another lyric.

For the next while they entertained themselves singing snippets of old tunes from those wild years and dancing up a storm along the path. Doubled over with laughter at one point, Stevie grabbed Kim's hands.

"This is the most fun I've had in forever," she said breathlessly. "Obviously I was too stuck in the kitchen, worrying about our business, for too long"

"And with good reason. You saved Cara Mia. But in the meantime, you forgot how it feels to let loose!" Kim threw her head back and let out a long "Woohooooo!"

They high fived and then pulled themselves together as a family of four came around a bend in the path. They greeted them with an enthusiastic *"Bonjour,"* stifling their giggles like a couple of school girls.

They needed to pay attention now, anyway, because a few metres farther on the path narrowed to accommodate only single-file walking. Fencing ensured no one would slip off into the water, but they could both see now why there was a warning not to take the trail in bad weather.

Close to the end of their three-kilometre hike, they came upon a private dock that jutted into the sea with a ladder at the end. They had been keeping their eyes open for it.

"Jean-Luc's instructions were right on the money," Kim said. "This is the place he recommended. He knows the property owner and they suggested we might take a dip."

They stripped down to bathing suits, descended the ladder and slipped into the crystal-clear water.

"Ahhh, this is heaven, perfection—soooo refreshing," Stevie sighed. "After so many days looking out at this sea, it feels amazing to be floating in it.

One end of the dock was sheltered by a rock wall that provided some shade. It was the perfect spot to enjoy the baguette sandwiches they had purchased at the market and the delicious triple brie Philippe had given them.

Feeling revitalized, they pulled on their shorts and tank tops and continued on to a sign that indicated the *sentier* had ended. The path led inland a short distance to a road, and suddenly a sweet, seductive fragrance filled the air. They had arrived at the rose garden entrance to the Belle Epoque gem, the Villa Eilenroc, built in 1867 and designed by Charles Garnier, architect of the Paris Opera.

Kim quickly googled its website and said, "We can't miss seeing this garden. It sounds spectacular. Full of roses, many of which were created right here in Antibes and Juan-les-Pins, which is the western part of Antibes now since the communities were joined. It says Antibes was famous as the rose capital of France back in the day, and that thousands of varieties are planted here."

In spite of the sweltering heat, time passed quickly. They followed paths that took them under bowers of climbing roses between one part of the enormous garden to the next, bending frequently to breathe in the variety of exotic scents and exclaiming about their heavenly perfumes. Eventually, in need of air conditioning, and seeing that the first floor of the villa was open to the public, they pulled rolled-up skirts from their backpacks and slipped them on over their shorts. Feeling more properly attired, they spent the next hour examining the intricate architectural details and stunning décor of the villa while listening to the audio guide through headphones.

It was easy for them to let their imaginations go wild and visualize the kind of life once lived so well in such a magnificent setting.

"Today has been an incredible experience," Stevie said, as they finished the tour. "From meeting Kat and Philippe to hiking this path and then being transported back more than a century."

"It all was very special, and sharing it with you made it all the more fun" Kim said with a grin.

Then she texted Bernadette, who replied she would be there within the half hour to collect them after she finished the job she was on. She suggested they walk the narrow lane that led from the villa up to a road. "There's a small café near there where you can wait and have something cool to drink."

CHAPTER 13

RETURN TO THE SHIP

Bernadette pulled up to the curb half an hour later, as promised, in her bright red Mercedes. She had inches to spare on each side of the car and the side mirrors were turned in. "Believe it or not, I can get down the narrowest lanes in this car. *J'adore!*"

She asked if Kim and Stephanie would like to see Juan Les Pins. "It's right here. The other half of Antibes and you really should see it. It's where all the action is at night."

Stephanie asked about the Hotel Belles Rives and Bernadette said, "*Mais oui!* Fitzgerald and Zelda and all the wild parties."

She drove them along one narrow road after another, all lined with villas peeking over the tops of walls and hedges, until they arrived in front of the hotel. "Here it is!" Bernadette said. "And there is the famous pine forest, La Pinède, where the Jazz à Juan started—and still plays. Always an exciting time in July! You must come back!"

She gave them a quick look at the golden strip of

sand that stretched to Cannes and pointed out her favorite beach restaurants. Then she drove them back across the Cap d'Antibes and headed to Nice.

Her enthusiasm was catching as she filled a good part of the drive along the Bord de Mer with stories from the past and juicy gossip from the present. She also regaled them with rebukes against French men—"ignorant smokers who like *pétanque* more than sex" and praise for les Suédois—"sexy Scandinavians who know how to treat a woman well."

It seemed in no time, they were pulling into the parking lot at the Vieux Port in Nice. Her sides sore from laughing, Kim tried to convince Bernadette to take payment for their ride.

"Non! Non! Eet's my geeft for Jean-Luc. He and Philippe are among the few French men I love. But remember—zat is how I feel. Lots and lots of women are crazy about French men. Don't limit yourself, you beautiful young travelers. Be open to everything on this adventure of yours. Come and visit us in Antibes again."

With a bise for both of them, and a wave out of the car window, Bernadette was on her way.

The ship was quiet as they made their way to their cabin, still laughing from their time with such a larger than life personality.

"So, remember Bernadette's message, Stevie, to be 'open to everything.'" Kim said, giving her a stern look that made them both laugh all over again.

Stevie's eye roll was affectionate. "She is certainly a woman who speaks her mind and knows what she wants. What a treat to meet her."

A small fruit plate was on their coffee table with a note from Liam that read, "The passengers won't return until later in the evening after their gourmet meal in Antibes.

Party in the crew dining room at 8—a seafood extravaganza with the best moules-frites ever. See you there!"

"Just enough time for a snooze and a shower," Kim said. "I'm feeling very salty!"

"Me too," Stevie said with a yawn. "I'm going to crash for an hour. Today was so awesome in every way! Antibes is the coolest—intriguing and beautiful. Definitely a town I want to revisit after the cruise."

"And now we have friends there! Kat and Philippe were so sincere," Kim added."

"She's from Toronto. How crazy is that? I loved her story. I admit she did give me a nudge about getting on with my life. Imagine the shock she must have had when her husband walked out!" Stevie flopped on her bed, phone in hand. "Today was a gamechanger for me ... a reminder that I have shut myself off from a lot of possibilities in life. Lesson learned! I've set the alarm for an hour and will be out like a light."

⚓

The crew party was in full swing when they walked in. Ryley, entertaining as always, was doing his mixologist thing and called them over to the bar.

"What'll it be, ladies? You look like you got some sun today—so something cool and refreshing—how about a Raspberry Gin Smash?"

"Yes, please," Kim said without hesitation. "That sounds irresistible."

"I'm going to be boring and have a rosé piscine," Stephanie said. "If I have any hard liquor tonight I'll be finished before I begin. After the day we had, I'm already a little drunk on sunshine and the stunning beauty of where we were."

"Ah, the Côte d'Azur has you under its spell! Drinking a rosé piscine like a local." Liam's voice reached them before he did as he made his way across the room. "It doesn't take long—especially if you take the route you did. Antibes will capture your heart."

He tapped his finger lightly on the large round wine glass in his other hand, which held rosé and ice cubes. "It truly is a refreshing drink. I agree." As soon as Stephanie was served her drink, he clinked her glass with his.

"So, let's hear all about your day. Jean-Luc told me he introduced you to Philippe and then you met his wife from Toronto. How cool a coincidence is that? And then he started you off on your hike. How did you like that *sentier*?"

Both women began talking at the same time, which caused more laughter. Then they found some chairs and gave Liam all the details.

As they chatted, a woman Stephanie recognized from the housecleaning staff came around with a large glass bowl filled with colorful paper fish.

"Hi, I'm Imogene," she said. "Take one of these fish, peel off the backing and stick it over your heart. There's a number on the fish and there will be a drawing for a special prize later. Also, your number identifies you in the karaoke contest. Good luck!"

"Karaoke?" Stephanie asked, wide-eyed. "I'm terrible. I truly cannot sing."

Liam assured her no one took it very seriously, but it was always a lot of fun.

Kim poked her and said, "Hey, we can do our Cyndi Lauper routine. Remember?"

"Ack! How could I forget?" Kim replied. "You've got to be kidding. We haven't done that since high school."

Liam's eyes shone. "I declare this is going to be good."

"Not going to happen," Stephanie insisted. "And I'm starving. Let's get some food."

They joined a table of ten. All the food was served family style. Platters of grilled fish, calamari and shrimp; heaping bowls of mussels with a choice of white wine sauce or curry sauce; and overflowing baskets of frites were just a few of the choices.

Carlos slid into a seat across from them with a beaming smile! "Kim. Estefania. Hola! I haven't seen you for days. Try the sardines and calamari. I've been grilling them for the last hour and we've got enough to feed an army!"

There were murmurs of satisfaction as everyone sampled the dishes.

Katherine, who had joined their table, exclaimed "This is crazy. I haven't seen this much seafood down here—ever. And everyone appears to be starving. Bon appétit!"

Glasses were raised with cheers of "Santé."

Kim nudged Stephanie. "Remember to look each person in the eye when you toast, the French way."

The level of conversation dropped as eating took precedence.

Soon, music was blaring and the crazy karaoke got under way. Champagne corks popped. The combination of music, laughter and alcohol created a high-energy atmosphere.

Stevie whispered to Kim at one point, "After all the sun we got this afternoon, these bubbles are going straight to my head."

Kim patted her on the head. "Don't worry. I've got your back, and after the fun we've had already, this might be the perfect way to finish the day. It's time to party!"

Stephanie grinned weakly. But she knew from experience that Kim always had a way of keeping things under control. She trusted that was still the case because she could feel herself slipping.

Before long Kim took the stage with her hair in two ponytails, leading a reluctant Stephanie by the hand. Monica handed them each a pair of outrageous oversized frame sunglasses, as prearranged by Kim.

Once the familiar opening glissando played, everyone knew what was coming and all the women leapt up to clap to Cyndi Lauper's famous anthem, "Girls Just Want to Have Fun." Soon they were singing along and bouncing up and down. It wasn't long before the men joined in dancing.

Kim kept encouraging them with shouts of "Time to partay!" and all of a sudden Stephanie let loose her rich auburn curls which, until that moment, she had tied back in a tight bun each day.

That action was greeted with cheers and applause, which only made Stephanie dance more energetically. A switch had been flipped, and she was giving in to spontaneous joy. It had been a long time coming.

A standing ovation caused Kim and Stephanie to do their Lauper routine again with even more enthusiasm and everyone was in stitches. Every act after theirs went out of their way to outdo the one before. It was nothing short of hilarious.

The evening's soundtrack followed a progression from the Rolling Stones to ABBA, Elton John, Bruno Mars, Beyoncé, Dua Lipa and Drake. By the end of the evening, all the crew knew each other and a strong bond amongst them developed.

As Liam walked Kim and Stephanie back to their room, he told them that the ship's administration had recognized many years ago that a karaoke night early in the cruise did a lot of good in building spirit amongst the crew.

Stephanie hiccupped loudly and leaned in to plant a sloppy kiss on Liam's cheek that was followed by a rather slurred endearment. "You're the besht!"

Liam chuckled as he bade them both a goodnight. "Thanks for helping to make the party so much fun!"

CHAPTER 14

BUONGIORNO PORTOFINO

Stephanie awoke with a start to the music of Cyndi Lauper. She moaned loudly and buried her head in her pillow.

"No! That's just cruel, Kim. Turn it off. There's no need for the reminder." Vague memories of their karaoke act sifted through her mind, accompanied by a hint of remorse. "Why did I let you talk me into that?"

Kim laughed and gave her shoulder a gentle shake. "I figured this was the best way to wake you up today. We're going to leave port in an hour and are expected to be out there mingling with the passengers."

Stevie groaned. "I'm not feeling great."

"No surprise there," Kim replied.

"How could you let me have so much to drink? You know that's not my style!"

"There was no stopping you last night! Once Cyndi got into your blood—and then all those ABBA songs got played—you were on a roll."

Stevie moaned even louder.

"Seriously, you were not out of control as you might think you were—not by a longshot. Besides, you know me. Mother Teresa when I need to be, otherwise we party. We had tons of fun, lots of laughs! You didn't drink very much. I think champagne simply goes to your head."

Kim handed her a fizzing liquid in a glass. "Here's an Alka Seltzer. It fixed us up back in the day and will do the same now."

Sitting up slowly and rubbing her eyes, Stevie took the glass and muttered, "That's a relief. Now I better jump in the shower. I'm so looking forward to being back in Italy—the homeland. This week in France has been an amazing adventure—so new to me in so many ways."

"You did love it," Kim agreed.

"But you know, as much as I try to get away from it, I'm ready for some Italian flavoring—and authentic Italian food for sure."

When she was dressed and waiting for Kim to finish with her makeup, Stevie turned on her phone notifications. A steady series of pings announced a lot of messages.

"Ooops – I'm getting fan messages for our act last night," Stevie said with a laugh as she flicked through them. Then her expression became serious. "But I don't know who sent this one. Listen. 'Hey Stephanie—I didn't realize who you were until you let your hair down, literally, last night. Those wild curls gave you away— StevieV's Pasta Party. I've been a fan for years. Are you traveling incognito here on purpose? Should I keep my mouth shut?'

She looked at Kim in desperation. "I've blown my cover! What am I going to do?"

"Who is it from?" Kim asked.

"The name is just Friendly Waiter. Should I answer this or ignore it?"

"Let's think about that. It's obviously someone in crew so I'm sure they don't mean any harm."

By the time they got to the main deck, it was already packed and mimosas were being served. Everyone cheered as the sails unfurled and the majestic first chords of Richard Strauss's "Also Spracht Zarathustra" filled the air. The ship glided off on its short trip along the Ligurian Coast of Italy to the harbour of Portofino, even smaller than that of Nice.

"As much as I fell in love with the coast of France and those cream-colored villages nestled in the hills, I'm even more drawn to these multi-colored pockets of buildings perched along this coast," Stevie told Kim. "It's a different vibe but still pulls me right in. I want to know who lives there. What do they do? What did they do through the centuries?"

"I know," Kim agreed. "It looks as if it would be impossible to reach some of those places. Imagine the drive!"

Monica stopped on her way by. "I've got to get back to waiting on the lunch bunch on the dining terrace," she said. "I just wanted to ask if you are coming with us for pasta in Portofino tonight."

"Si! Sounds great!" Kim replied. "And Liam

mentioned the new Italian chef will come on board there today or tomorrow as well. I'm excited!"

After Monica went on her way, Stevie said, "Explain to me again why the Italian chef is just joining now? Is that usually the way things go? They wait until Italy for him to join?"

Kim shook her head. "No, it's not usual. I got the skinny on it at the party the other night. You were already into your karaoke persona so I didn't talk to you about it then. You never would have remembered—nor would you have been interested at that point." She laughed out loud and then snorted. "Ooops—sorry—but you were so damn funny."

Stevie crossed her eyes and put her hands over her face. "Please spare me the details."

Kim brushed her hand lightly across her face and assumed a serious expression. "In answer to your question, on the previous cruise, all the chefs were on board from the beginning. Apparently, the Italian chef who was booked for this cruise had a heart attack right before he was supposed to embark in Barcelona. This guy who is coming is a friend of Captain Keeling and apparently he has spent some time testing new recipes on some previous trips through the years. I hear his cooking is legendary! He lives in Portofino. So management made a decision to pick him up there. That's the scoop."

She had the Google link to the chef's website in a file on her phone and texted it to Stevie.

"Emilio Romano. I read about him when I was at the cooking school in Florence. He has such an impressive history. The food will be amazing. He must come with an entourage."

"Yup. Someone said he brings along his own sous chef."

Stevie's eyes lit up. "So far, the food here has been excellent, but when this guy gets in the kitchen, we are all going to be in for a real treat. I wonder why he would even want to work on a ship. There must be more to the story."

"A bit of mystery, you think? From what I gathered he's doing it just as a favor to the Captain. Liam will know the deets." Kim said.

"Liam doesn't seem to be a gossip, so it will be interesting to see if he says anything."

"Good thing we have some strenuous hikes planned in the coming weeks. The one thing I don't want to own at the end of this cruise is more flab."

They both laughed and pulled horror-stricken expressions.

"And now we better get to work," Kim said as she opened the cabin door. "You know that line I showed you that I created with the epidote stones sent to me from Italy during lockdown? Well, today's the day we roll it out."

"Sounds good. I'd never heard of that stone until you showed the pieces to me the other day," Stevie said.

As soon as they got to the shop, Kim took a tray out from the locked storage counter, and explained why she had chosen only the pistachio-like green colored epidotes even though she also had amber shades.

"I think having all the same color in varying shades

makes for a more effective display. I really dove into research about it and learned that green represents life, renewal and calmness. This stone has a reputation for being chakra balancing."

"Ha!" Stephanie said wryly. "My chakra could definitely use some balancing. But you are right, that's an impressive display."

Kim leaned over to Stephanie and placed a green teardrop-shaped pendant on a silver chain around her neck.

"Oh, am I going to model pieces today?" Stevie asked.

"No. This is for you. From me. It will hang right by your heart and work its magic. I just know it will."

Stevie gasped. "Kimster. Not necessary. I can buy it!"

"Nope!" Kim held up her hand. "It won't mean the same. I need this to be from me to you. I made it with love for you and for the love that is waiting somewhere for you."

Kim's eyes glistened as Stevie hugged her and said, "No crying—but I'm crying inside. This is so beautiful in so many ways. Thank you, my dearest, bestest friend."

Kim cleared her throat. "Okay, here we go. Showtime! The ladies will be excited!"

Kim was right. All afternoon, there was at least one and often a group of customers at their counter, and all of them were completely taken by the soft green shades of the epidote stones and crystals. Several already were familiar with the history of it being associated with the heart chakra. The afternoon at the boutique turned into something of a healing session as various women shared stories about the epidote crystal's power to generate hope.

Maya, the ship's yoga and fitness instructor, gasped when she stopped by and saw the display. "This stone speaks to me in so many ways," she said to the women gathered around. She extended her left hand to show a simple pinky ring set with small epidote crystals. "I can't wear anything big when I'm working, but I never take this off."

Martha Francescatto sidled up beside Maya at the counter. "I was admiring that in yoga class the other day. It's simple and elegant. What a coincidence to see this jewelry here."

"Thanks," Maya replied as she held her hand out for the others to admire. Many women exclaimed loudly.

"Honestly," Annie, a passenger from Long Island, said breathlessly, pointing to the bracelet on her wrist. "I know my bracelet of epidote stones changed my life. From the moment I began wearing it, my energy level increased. I found the strength to speak my intentions out loud and make them happen. I'm so thrilled to buy more jewelry with epidotes!"

And she did, along with so many others that the entire epidote collection sold out. Kim promised there would be another shipment waiting for her when they docked in a few days. She made a hurried call to her accountant in Toronto who was also her next-door neighbour and arranged for a box to be shipped.

By four o'clock passengers were gathered back on the deck as the *Dream Maker*, almost in slow motion, rounded a cape in the rocky coastline and the romantic, colorful tiny harbor of Portofino lay before them. Magnificent villas hugged the steep hill that was crowned by a splendid castle.

The effect was instantaneous. Sighs were audible. Couples embraced.

An earlier announcement had explained to everyone that no music would be played this time. Instead Liam's melodic accent wafted through the ship's speakers. "The spectacular first sight of magnificent Portofino is all we need to lift our hearts—and besides that its residents do not appreciate loud music—or loud anything. Please remember to be extra respectful in this very special town."

He paused for a moment to not interfere with the strong visual effect of the scenery before them. Then he continued, "As you know, this is a tender port, which means you will all be transported to the main square in our tenders. It will take us a little while but enjoy the short ride. We are all blessed to be here. Passengers signed up for a moonlit dinner at the Hotel Splendido should be ready to begin leaving the ship at seven p.m. Horse-drawn carriages will be waiting in the piazzetta to carry you up the hill to the hotel. I promise you a fine experience."

Kim explained to Stevie that a "tender port" meant one too small for any ships to dock in—even the *Dream*

Maker. "So we go in the little boats we have, the tenders. And by the by, there are no horse-drawn carriages for us peasants."

Stevie chuckled.

"But we have the pleasure of eating in town," Katherine said. She had joined them minutes before. "It's not *the* Splendido—but it *is* splendido! Take my word for it! Catch you around eight. for our turn to leave the ship."

CHAPTER 15

PERFECT PORTOFINO

As they changed to go into town for dinner, Stevie said to Kim, "Could we have found a better salesperson today than Maya? She was wonderful. So sincere. And then how about Annie? Bonus!"

"The best. Thank goodness I had more inventory at home. I had a feeling this line would be a big seller—but never *this* big! Did you notice that Martha bought a piece as well?"

"She is one cool lady! We chatted a bit today, but things were so busy there wasn't much time. She asked if we were going to hike in Cinque Terre and I told her our plans."

"Great! Perhaps she will go with us. I really enjoyed her company at Èze."

Stevie nodded with a grin. "Me too! But in answer to your question about Annie, if she is right, I may never take this pendant off."

Kim chuckled.

"By the way," Stevie continued, "have I said thank you and that I love you and this amazing gift?"

Kim waved her hand, brushing off the thanks. "Only a bazillion times. Enough already! I'm so glad you love it." Her voice caught as she added. "I want that stone to work its magic on you."

Stevie hugged her. "That is so sweet. So are you. I could use a little magic, and I have a sense just being back in Italy will help. I didn't want to whine but I've been feeling the need for some true *sugo*. My body is telling me it's missing that special something in our sauce."

Kim frowned. "You should have said something. I'm sorry that's been bothering you."

"Hey," Stevie replied, shaking her head. "It's not that serious. Just a nagging awareness from time to time that something is missing in my psyche. I'm not thinking about Benny much anymore but I am thinking about cooking Italian. I think I'll be ready to go back to the kitchen when my time on the ship is over." She rubbed the tattoo on her wrist.

Kim nodded and looked into her eyes with the understanding that only comes from years of "bestfriend-ship," as they called it. "We both know the kitchen is your first love. And we know you will get back to it after our little hiatus. Now we need to hurry, though, so we can catch the tender to the harbour."

Stevie checked herself in the mirror and picked up a shawl she had laid on her bed. "Ready! I'm keen to ride into the harbour in that motor boat. I'm still blinking from that first view of Portofino. Imagine! It's just like all the stunning photos I've seen for years."

"Picture-postcard pretty. There's no other way to describe it." Kim agreed.

The tender dropped Stephanie and their party of eight on the south side of the harbour near stairs leading up to the castle. From there it was just a few minutes stroll to the main cobblestone *piazzetta*. Multi-colored, four and five story houses rimmed the square. Laundry lines stretched from one window to another indicated that families still made their homes in the centuries-old buildings.

Restaurants lined the side of the harbour where they were strolling, each with a terrace that spread out into the walkway. Men and women were sitting at small tables and standing in the spaces between, holding wine glasses and chatting animatedly. Gentle laughter heightened the air of merriment that prevailed. It was party time on the patio.

Stevie felt like a true tourist as she gaped, open-mouthed at the timeworn buildings and imagined the lives that had lived there over so many centuries. Suddenly she bumped into someone and something wet splashed over her dress, accompanied by a shout of "*Attenta!*" as a man jumped aside, his wine glass empty.

She found herself looking into the annoyed but seductive green eyes of an attractive man about her age. It was impossible for her not to notice his striking olive skin and dark hair.

"*Scusa!*" she said. "*Non l'aveyo visto.*" Her first reaction was to reply in Italian, but she switched immediately to English. "I didn't see you!"

The stranger began a tirade in Italian, but stopped abruptly and also switched to English. "Obviously you weren't looking. Open your eyes!"

A waiter rushed over with napkins to help and attended to them both. He spoke in a more respectful way to the man, making it apparent he was well known. Stevie felt most definitely brushed off as a tourist.

"I'm so, so sorry," she apologized again. "Thank goodness it is white wine!" But then she noticed, to her horror, the dark stain spreading over his fashionably tailored pale blue linen sports jacket, white shirt and even his khaki pants.

She wondered how such a mess came from one glass of wine as she mumbled "*Scusa*" again.

The young man's gaze hardened and he muttered to his friends, who nodded and chuckled. Stephanie only heard the word "*turista*" and her face turned beet red.

She had been lagging behind the rest of her group, and only Liam had noticed the incident. He made certain Stevie was ok and whisked her away, leaving a trail of apologies for the man and his group.

"I feel like an idiot!" she grumbled to Liam, as he held her arm and walked her briskly along the quay.

"Ach, accidents happen. No worries. Some fresh pasta will make everything right again," Liam said, offering comfort.

⚓

Liam's prediction was spot on. Dinner was delicious.

And it drove Stephanie crazy. This was her world. Her aromas. Her tastes. And she had to be quiet about it. Her choice.

It began with the antipasti served on an enormous hand-painted platter, shared by the group. Mixed cured meats, warm olives, and grilled Mediterranean vegetables were artfully displayed. Each bite elicited murmurs of pleasure all around the table.

The next course, the *primi*, was a traditional pasta with everyone making their own choice. Stephanie's linguine was light and with just the right stage of *al dente* firmness. Her mind flicked back longingly to her TikTok posts and she could feel some melancholy setting in. She knew before she even tasted it that the sauce would be delicious—the aroma of spices rising from it was divine —but the effect was not even close compared to Paola's recipe. That secret ingredient was missing.

Secondi was baked sea bass with the side dish— the *contorno*—seasonal asparagus with lemon, and grilled potatoes. Some chose the vegetarian option.

Frutta was a mixed fruit salad and dessert a choice between tiramisù, panna cotta, or cannoli. Stevie knew the tiramisù would be safest for her. She had a few memories tied up in that basic desert. An assortment was ordered and everyone dug in.

The meal took several enjoyable hours to eat, and was accompanied by lively conversation and laughter. Just being in a true Italian trattoria awakened thoughts and feelings Stevie had tucked away when she made the decision to go on the cruise. She wondered if it was safe to let them out now. Could she rein them in again? she asked herself.

To top the meal off, their server offered them a glass of limoncello "on the house," and the group stumbled out reluctantly around midnight after calling for a tender. Some of the guys attempted serenading in Italian, which had Liam shushing everyone as they stifled their giggles.

Stephanie was quiet on the short ride back to the ship, wrapped up in a swirl of memories from her own kitchen. A deep desire was simmering inside her. She could feel it. Taste it. She needed to get it under control.

Liam slipped into the seat beside her. "I didn't know you spoke Italian."

She thought quickly and replied, "Just bits and pieces remembered from my grandmother and my high school courses. Those words just popped out automatically when I bumped into that guy."

"What guy?" Kim asked. "What did I miss?"

"Oh my God," Stephanie said. "Talk about embarrassing! There was a group of guys standing on the terrace drinking wine as we walked to the restaurant. I was so busy gawking at all the quaintness, I wasn't paying attention and bumped into one. Spilled his wine all over him. He was not pleased."

Liam added that the fellow had not been kind to Stephanie and had called her a tourist. "All of his mates had a good laugh over it."

Stephanie gulped. "Why wouldn't they? I knocked a big glass of wine all over his shirt, jacket and pants. Then I mumbled and fumbled like an idiot. Really did a number! But—mmmm—he had the most gorgeous eyes —and hair and skin. It was almost worth it to get a good look at him."

Liam chuckled.

"And thank you, Liam, for rescuing me as though I were a damsel in distress!"

Chapter 16

Surprise!

The following day was a quiet one on board ship as most passengers were on an all-day tour of the town of Portofino, the castle and surrounding stunning countryside. An al fresco lunch was being served in the fields at a vineyard.

Stephanie offered to dust and clean all the displays in the afternoon, while Kim worked at a counter putting together beaded necklaces and bracelets.

"It works well having the time in port to prepare for being open for business when we are at sea," Stephanie said.

Kim murmured her agreement and added, "But what works best is having you here with me. I'm so grateful you came along."

Stephanie reached out and gave her a squeeze on the shoulder. "You saved me! Funny how things work out sometimes, isn't it? I mean, who knew we would find ourselves doing this together?"

Stephanie also took advantage of the time to have

some long text conversations with her parents and Nonna Bella. Most days she exchanged simple messages and a photo or two in the evening.

Today they were texting in real time and could respond immediately. They had time to describe what they had been doing while she was gone. They were all in agreement that the break from the trattoria was giving them time to relax and recuperate.

Then her mom and Bella called on WhatsApp.

"Enough of this texting," Bella said. "This is so much easier."

She told Stephanie she had been working on some new recipes from time to time. "I miss you by my side in the kitchen, *mio tesoro*. But what news—Chef Romano! This is unbelievable. His family is from Bisnonna Paola's village. I am familiar with his cousins there. Mamma mia!"

"Dio mio! I want to say something to him. Do you think he will know I'm a chef? I'm not sure I want him to know. Have you spoken to his cousins recently?" Stevie tried to contain her excitement.

"I've tried several of his recipes, and you may learn some good ideas from him," Bella said. Then she changed the subject. "Are you not doing your Pasta Party on the TikTok? I've been watching out for you."

Stevie felt it was time to tell the Angels and Bella that she was hiding from her cooking history and keeping it a secret. She had worried they would not understand.

"We do understand," her mother said. "Bella too. We know you needed to get away and have a change and that's okay. But this is kind of an interesting coincidence.

Perhaps you can speak to Chef Romano in confidence. Think about it."

"I am getting out the cards," Bella said. "This definitely calls for a reading and I will tell you what I discover."

They said goodbye with love and positive messages. "We are so happy you made the decision to go on this trip," Angela said. "You sound full of life again. Give our love to Kim."

Stephanie felt as though she might burst from happiness after their conversation.

Then she felt a pang of guilt about keeping her true identity a secret on the ship. But she knew that was how she wanted to live her life at this moment. Incognito. Even though the lure of the kitchen was growing stronger.

She relayed her family's messages to Kim as well as the surprising connection with Chef Romano.

"Wow! That's amazing," Kim said. "You should definitely tell him and see how he responds."

The passengers began to arrive back later in the day, and a few women came by the shop. They were entranced watching Kim at work and asked if she would do a workshop with them. She told Stevie later that the good supply of beads she had brought with her was in case the opportunity arose to do just that.

"A good entrepreneurial move, my friend!" Stevie said. "The way those women responded to the pieces you have done today tells me they will be snapped up in no time."

Kim laughed. "Maybe we should go into business

together when we get back home, if you still feel you need a change."

Stevie chuckled. Then she was quiet for a moment. "Don't get me wrong. I'm having a lot of fun doing this with you. But one thing I'm realizing as days go by is how much I miss being in the kitchen. I'm starting to feel I will be happy to be back at Cara Mia in another few weeks—even if I have no one to go home to afterward."

"Stevie, we know cooking is in your blood. In your soul! Remember when the rest of us girls were playing with dolls, you just wanted to be in the kitchen with Paola and Bella making pasta. You come by it honestly."

Stevie nodded slowly.

Kim put her hands on her friend's shoulders. "And as for going home alone—girl! Give love a chance. This time on your own can only make your life better. You will know it when the real thing comes along. I know you will." Then she pulled her in for a long hug, returned with equal emotion.

"One thing I know for sure, Kimster, I do love you!"

"And I love you, Stevie-boo! We will always have each other."

They stepped back and gave each other a high-five that ended with a pinkie grip, as they had done as far back as they could remember.

That evening as they were getting ready to go to dinner, Stevie showed Kim a text message she had received. The mysterious sender was still asking why she did not want anyone to know about her TikTok account and real identity.

"Whoever it is doesn't seem threatening," she said.

"No" Kim agreed. "Just curious—and even admiring. Hmmm, a mystery man?"

"Or woman," Stevie added. "Who knows? Do you think I should continue to ignore them?"

Kim shrugged. "Let's see if it continues. Maybe the person will take the hint when you don't respond."

Stephanie wrinkled her nose. "I'm torn. If the person is just being nice, I feel badly ignoring their texts. But I don't want to encourage anything either."

"Well don't do anything now, as we better get to the main dining room," Kim said. "Captain Keeling is going to introduce Chef Romano and the special Flavors of Italy menu he has created for the next ten days. Liam said they are live streaming it to the crew dining room too but I want to be there in person."

"Me too. He's a true celebrity in my books," Stevie gushed. "And a relative too. Who knew?"

The main dining area was filled with passengers, as well as the outside dining terrace beyond it. Large video screens had been carefully placed so everyone had a good view of the captain's presentation.

Liam waved them over to his table where he was holding two of ten seats for them. They had an excellent view of the Captain's table where the guest of honor was seated and other people Stevie did not recognize.

Captain Keeling called for everyone's attention and introduced the star of the evening.

Chef Emilio Romano was a tall, white-haired man with movie-star good looks and a most charming Italian accent. He spoke about his longstanding friendship with Captain Keeling and how he joined one of these cruises from time to time to test new recipes.

"I hope you are ready for a gustatorial adventure—could be at breakfast, lunch or dinner. I know many evenings you are on land for a meal, and that is when I get to plan and create for the next time I have you as my captive diners." His laugh was smooth and melodious. Stevie watched the faces of women, who were being drawn in by his easy magnetism. A few of them were almost swooning as he spoke about his menus and the joy of preparing food he'd experienced since he was a child.

"I'm joining the swooners," Stevie whispered to Kim. "He speaks directly to my heart and—oh my gawd—" She stopped speaking abruptly, picked up the large paper menu on her table and hid behind it.

Kim looked at her in surprise and then back to Chef Romano as he was introducing his sous chef, a handsome young man whose name was Maximus, although everyone called him Max. Emilio explained. "He is my nephew and runs his own tiny trattoria in Venice. Often when I do this cruise, he leaves his shop and joins me. We are collaborators and I promise you dishes that will leave you clamoring for more!"

Max flashed a brilliant smile, enhanced by his wavy black hair, dark olive skin and sparkling green eyes. He bowed slightly and acknowledged the room but stepped back, clearly not interested in remaining in the limelight.

The room darkened and a short video followed that detailed the highlights of Chef Emilio's career. It also told the history of Max learning his craft in the kitchens of his uncle since he was a small boy. When the lights came back on, both men had disappeared but the room still erupted in applause.

Captain Keeling held the floor once again. "There you have it, my friends. I'm delighted that you are on board to experience this unique opportunity. Tomorrow our menus will begin to feature the special Italian offerings Chef Romano spoke of this evening. Please enjoy the rest of your meal and tomorrow be ready to begin each one with buon appetite—with gusto!"

Kim turned to Stevie and was surprised that she was breathing heavily and still hiding behind the menu.

"Stephanie, what's going on?" Kim asked, keeping her voice to a whisper.

Stevie seemed on the verge of hyperventilating. "Th... th...that's him!" she gasped.

Liam reached over and patted Stephanie's hand. "Funny how things happen, my dear. What a coincidence! But he probably doesn't remember it was you."

"Will you tell me what you are talking about?" Kim asked in exasperation

"He's the guy I spilled wine all over last night!" Stevie blurted. "This is going to be so embarrassing! Of all people!"

She fanned herself with the paper menu. "*Porca vacca*! Holy cow!" she muttered. "What the fuck?"

CHAPTER 17

GOING INCOGNITO

Kim gently lifted the top sheet on the mound on Stevie's bed and peeked in. "Okay. You can't hide there all day long. Rise and shine."

"I know. I know. I'm working on how to get through the day," Stevie responded in a muted voice, as she pulled the sheet back over her head.

Kim sat on the bed. "Well then, what's the plan? I have a feeling you want me to bring your breakfast here."

"You are an angel—absolutely right! You know I don't want much but I have a good idea of what Italian treats will be on the buffet. Please bring me a maritozzi."

"They are the ones filled with whipped cream, right?"

Stevie groaned. "Just the thought of one of those makes me ecstatic. Bella makes the best."

"No problem! Here's your espresso," Kim said as she lifted the cover again and held the cup under it to let the rich aroma waft in.

Stevie sat up and took the cup. "Grazie," she whispered. "This will help kick me into gear."

Their morning at the boutique was busy as word had spread about the new beaded pieces Kim had created. This was a lay-away only day since they were still in port and that always took more time organizing.

Later that day, most of the passengers would be leaving for a twelve-course dinner at the most famous restaurant in Portofino. It seemed no one wanted to miss out on choosing pieces to put away before it was all spoken for. It was so busy, it took some time before Kim noticed that Stevie was still wearing the dark sunglasses she'd put on before they left their cabin.

"Stephanie, are you going to wear those sunglasses all day?" Kim asked, in a lull between customers.

"Well, yeah—I don't want to take the chance of Max recognizing me. I'm not ready to be humiliated," she said. "When anyone asks, I've told them I have a migraine and wearing these really helps me. Everyone so far has been understanding and sympathetic."

Kim stifled a serious case of the giggles. "You crack me up! So, has your nemesis been around at all?"

Stevie shook her head. "A couple of times I thought I caught a glimpse. But they were false alarms, and believe me I have been on high alert."

Not long afterward, Martha dropped by with lattes for both of them. "I took a chance these might be a good treat about now."

"Thanks," Kim said. "Coffee will hit the spot!"

Stephanie lifted hers in agreement.

"How's the migraine?" Martha asked. "I heard that

you are suffering from one today, and I know how debilitating they can be."

Stevie kept her voice low, hoping she sounded a bit fragile. "It's there but improving. Thanks for asking."

After chatting about how exciting it was to have Emilio Romano on board, Martha said, "And how about that handsome nephew of his? I understand he has his uncle's magic touch in the kitchen, as well as being to-die-for gorgeous!"

"Totally agree," Kim said. "I can't wait for their first dinner menu tomorrow night!"

"Chef Romano is one of my heroes," Stephanie said.

"And you have nothing to say about Maximus?" Martha asked.

Stephanie tried to look uninterested. "Well, I don't know anything about his cooking and his looks don't do anything for me. Not my type."

Martha gave her a quizzical look and changed the subject. "Are you interested in walking up to the castle this afternoon, once the ship empties for the mega eat-a-thon? It's the best place to take photos of the town."

Kim said she was going to stay and keep working on her beading. "It's too good an opportunity to make more new pieces. Once I get into it I don't want to stop. I'm telling you, beading is addictive. But I love it."

"And your designs are spectacular! No wonder everyone is interested in them," Martha exclaimed.

Stephanie grinned. "While Kim is working her magic, I would love to do that walk with you."

"That would be lovely, but do you think you are well enough?" Martha asked.

Stephanie gulped and hoped she sounded convincing. "I'm feeling a lot better already, thanks. Wearing these glasses really does help."

Kim looked away so Martha would not see her struggle to keep her face composed.

Stephanie kept the sunglasses on for the entire morning, and a few times Kim caught her dropping down behind a counter when she thought she saw Max approaching. She had laughed the first time they were alone when Stevie ducked.

"Pure paranoia," Stevie had muttered. "Good thing I'm going out with Martha this afternoon."

A few hours later, Stevie and Martha were climbing a narrow staircase of worn stones leading from the marina, where the tender had dropped them. Still wearing her sunglasses and having added a wide-brimmed straw hat pulled low on her forehead, Stephanie fit right in with the other tourists.

As they hiked, she told Martha how she had been overwhelmed by the loveliness of the village when they walked to dinner the night before. "The simple beauty of it is the stuff of dreams. So untouched, it seems."

At the top of the stairs, they followed a winding trail to Castello Brown, a stone fortress from the fifteenth century. Martha offered a brief history lesson.

"This spot has been fortified for harbour defence since Roman times. Apparently, Richard the Lionheart stayed here for a while on his way to the Third Crusade."

Stevie felt the familiar rush that this kind of history gave her.

"After the sixteen hundreds, when battles died down, it became more of a place to find refuge," Martha continued. "Like so many sites like this it was abandoned in the nineteenth century before later being purchased and restored in stages. Now it belongs to the local government."

"That's really interesting," Stephanie exclaimed. "It's so cool to actually be places which have a long history. It's one of the reasons I loved living in Italy when I was at cooking school and the few times I visited with my family. It's good to be back."

"Exactly my feelings," Martha agreed. "I never tire of it. Oh, and for a bit of more modern history, in 1922, Elizabeth von Arnim wrote her novel *The Enchanted April* here. It became the movie *Enchanted April*. You're probably too young to have seen it."

"I loved that movie! My Italian great-grandmother and grandmother had me watch it with them —at least five times," Stephanie said with a chuckle.

"Then you know its uplifting theme of hope and love," Martha said, her voice soft, as she looked deeply into Stevie's eyes, despite the dark glasses.

Stevie was touched by the gentle calm of Martha's gaze and sensed its message. She'd hoped her depression hadn't been that transparent. They held their connection, and Stephanie nodded as the words went straight to her heart. She knew deep inside she did want to feel hopeful about love. She just had to get to a point where she acknowledged it and opened her heart.

The moment was lightened when Martha added, "It was filmed right here in the nineties."

"It was such a beautiful story. We always had a box of tissues to pass around—and the scenery was spectacular," Stephanie said.

"Well, there you go," Martha said. "Recognize that?" She gestured to a perfect vantage point between trees. Before her was the most-photographed view of the village and harbour with the sparkling sea and the lushly forested hills unfolding behind.

Stevie took off her sunglasses and stuck them around her hat. She sighed as she snapped photos, using both her phone and her camera. "These are perfect views, Martha. Thank you for bringing me up here."

She lowered her camera to take in the brilliant turquoise of the water. Boats of all sizes bobbed in the tiny harbour. Overflowing flowerboxes and lines of laundry hung from tall, colourful houses clustered around the marina and the piazzetta. A long sigh escaped her lips.

Martha smiled at her. "It's so romantic, isn't it? You should be here with a handsome young Italian and not someone old enough to be your grandmother."

Stephanie's mouth pressed into a wry grin. "That's not in my cards these days. Romance is not on my agenda."

She leaned back on the bench where they had taken a seat, sighed and nodded but uttered nothing more. But sensing romance and love in the air all around her made her realize she had not felt either in her life for several years. Nada. And now she worried that desire like that might be lost to her forever.

Martha looked at her and said, "Stephanie, I hope you don't mind if I tell you something."

"Of course not," Stephanie said, wondering what on earth it might be.

"I know who you are. I know your grandmother Bella very well and have eaten at your trattoria many times through the years," Martha said.

Stevie's jaw dropped and she blinked in amazement. "You're kidding!"

"No, I'm not," Martha said, smiling warmly. "Bella and I were on the same volunteer committee at the Church of Mary and Joseph. I liked her very much—and loved eating at Cara Mia. I remember seeing dear Paola there too. And I watched you grow up! I didn't say anything before because I felt you did not want to be recognized."

Stephanie looked at her, embarrassed. "You guessed correctly. I'm so sorry. I don't recognize you."

"You wouldn't. Before Covid I had long brown hair with highlights. This white hair has been my new look for two years now."

Stephanie smiled back at Martha, her immediate alarm vanishing thanks to Martha's gracious manner. "What an incredible coincidence."

"It's a small world. You realize that more and more as life goes on," Martha said. "As I recall, your grandmother told me you and your high school sweetheart were a number. Don't you wish he was here?"

Stephanie shook her head slowly. "Speaking of

history, as we were, the sweetheart belongs in that category. It's another part of the reason I'm here losing myself on the Med."

Martha gave her a sympathetic pat on the arm. "Oh, I'm sorry to have brought that up."

"It's okay, really. It's one of those things that probably should have happened a long time ago. But, you know—Covid messed up a lot of things in life—and I think the inevitable just got delayed."

"You are a beautiful, talented young woman. There will be someone very special out there waiting for you," Martha said, her eyes kind and sincere.

Stephanie touched her tattoo without thinking. "That's what Bisnonna Paola used to say to me. She urged me to come back to Italy to find true love. Now I'm here in the perfect place—but ..."

She looked at Martha and they both burst out laughing.

"Not that you aren't good company," Stephanie continued.

"Ha! Time for a glass of vino. We can walk a bit farther up to the lighthouse. There's a café there—at least there was the last time I was here. Who knows, these days?"

They continued walking, breathing in the fragrant air of the lush flowering shrubs that bordered the path. Bees were buzzing and butterflies fluttering in perfect harmony.

Stephanie stumbled over a few loose rocks and was impressed with Martha's agility as she seemed to have no trouble. She felt she was not in nearly as good shape as the older woman and vowed to pay more attention to her conditioning. Soon they reached the small lighthouse where more photo ops presented themselves.

"Is it any wonder," Martha asked, gazing around at all the couples wandering arm in arm and stopping to kiss, "that so many people come here to get married? The entire village and setting simply ooze romance, don't they?"

Then she changed the subject. "Stephanie, don't worry. I won't betray your secret and tell anyone who you are. But, please you must give Bella my warm regards."

"I will! What a small world. And you are right. When I decided to come along to help Kim sell her jewelry, I didn't want anyone to know I was a chef. I'm having a hiatus from my real life ..." Her voice dropped and she hesitated.

"And if I may be so bold, you're suffering from a broken heart too. I can read it in your eyes, hear it in your voice," Martha interjected.

"You're right on that count too. It seemed to be the perfect opportunity for me to figure out what I want to do with my life."

"Don't give up on love, my dear. You are young with a lifetime to fill ahead of you."

"About to turn thirty, doesn't feel like young," Stephanie murmured.

Martha scoffed. "My girl, you are still in your youth at thirty. Trust me. You're just beginning to reach your real power. You millennials all think your twenties were the best time—and I'm sure they were good years—but now you are on the brink of really being able to experience life. Everything you did and learned in the last decade has made you smarter and stronger and you can be confident now. Enjoy the ride of your thirties."

She ended with a smile so warm and knowing, Stephanie felt awash in sudden optimism.

"I feel you are speaking from experience, Martha," she said, and Martha nodded. Her eyes sparkled with reminiscence.

"I remember fondly, and some not so fondly, several love affairs in my early twenties, before I married Robert. But I knew when I met him that nothing compared to what we shared. Then we were fortunate to have a happy marriage for almost sixty years. You will know when the real thing comes along, my dear. Trust me."

They sat in large wicker chairs strategically placed to protect them from the blazing sun. Strong scents from the surrounding flower-filled garden sweetened the air.

The waiter brought a small pitcher of prosecco and poured some carefully into two flutes. The women raised their glasses and toasted each other. "*Alla salute!*" and "*Cin cin!*"

They sat back in the comfortable chairs, letting the ambiance of the setting wrap around them.

"I'm going to close my eyes for a few minutes," Martha said. "This is the perfect place for a quick catnap."

"Be my guest," Stephanie said. "I've got lots to catch up with on my phone." The first thing she did was text Bella and the Angels and tell them about Martha.

To her dismay, she noticed another anonymous text had arrived It read, "Don't worry! I'm not trying to embarrass you and won't say anything, but why won't you tell everyone who you are? I am sure there are others here who follow you."

She thought about blocking the number but did not want to worsen the situation. Whoever it was seemed to be nice.

After a while, she walked to a nearby stone wall and sat overlooking the remarkable view and thought about Martha's words. Could she really feel that confidence in herself now? She wondered if that kind of romance would be part of her life. She wasn't sure that she even wanted it. The risk of having her heart broken again just seemed too much to bear.

CHAPTER 18

THE INEVITABLE

Chef Emilio Romano's first menu reveal was a spectacular event. The dining areas were decorated in green, white and red and Italian flags were raised everywhere. Everyone had been encouraged to dress in the same colors as well. Italian music played and the atmosphere was celebratory.

A decorated menu set at each place gave an extensive description of each course and information about Chef Romano's own Michelin-starred restaurant in Naples.

In his introduction of Chef Romano to the passengers, Captain Keeling had stressed that the next ten days would bring their very own Michelin-starred restaurant to the ship. All the way to Sicily.

During the lively evening, Chef Romano and his nephew, Max, visited every table in the main dining areas to listen to people's comments and answer their questions.

Stephanie was dying to speak to Emilio but did not want to draw attention to herself. When the chef, trailed by Max, appeared to be approaching their table, she vanished to the lady's room.

"Whew! Made it safely through tonight," she said to Kim as they went to their cabin later. "We can eat in the crew dining room until this excitement dies down."

Kim said, "No way I'm going to miss all the hoopla and fabulous food. And neither are you. I know the food will be served in the crew area too but not in the same fashion. You've got to put your big girl panties on and get over this."

Stephanie pulled a face but then smiled. "You are right. Besides, I'm sure there are some attractive young babes in the kitchen who would be happy to see Max."

"And some not so young, cool older women passengers who would be happy to get to know him better," Kim added. "Or his uncle. Oooh là là."

Stephanie's eyes glazed over and she murmured, "Max is so gorgeous he probably has a stunning Italian beauty waiting for him to come home."

She climbed onto her bed and lost herself in a new cookbook she had downloaded recently. The exquisite descriptions of pasta and sauces would be her romance.

The next morning, the ship left Portofino and cruised along the coast, giving passengers astonishing views of the Cinque Terre region and the five multicolored, hillside fishing villages that tumbled to the sea. Liam joined Stephanie and Kim on deck and described how these ancient communities were originally linked together through the surrounding steep slopes by paths shaped by shepherds and donkeys. Then after WWI, when tourism grew in the area, hiking trails were created along these timeworn paths. Later a rail line was built to link the villages with the outside world.

Stephanie loved learning that these trails, now famous for hikers, were once the only way for people living in the villages to connect, unless by boat. She thought how it must have been incredibly difficult to get around, but the romance of it all stayed with her.

Martha, in what Stephanie now appreciated as her usual gentle, caring way, had joined them and talked about her own hiking experiences in the area.

The ship was anchored offshore for the day, and passengers were invited to hike part or all of the trail, known as the Verde Azzurro path. Tenders would take them to one of three of the villages, depending on how long a hike they wanted. Some passengers chose to walk the six-hours trail that connected all five villages, while others chose a short portion.

After careful consideration, Stephanie and Kim decided to hike the easy, but storied Via dell'Amore, the Way of Love between Riomaggiore and Manarola, a thirty-minute walk on a wide, paved path that had just been reopened after several years of repairing damage caused by landslides.

Armed with sunscreen, hats and water, they left on the first tender as the sun was just beginning to warm the air. Seeing lineups already beginning to form at the various sightseeing booths, they picked up their ticket and were glad to set off.

Kim said, "Oh man! We got here just in time. Look at that tour group coming behind us. Let's get moving!"

"Well, this should be quite a simple stroll but I can see it would be a super drag to do it when it is packed with people," Stephanie observed.

Portions of the walk were carved right out of the cliffs and hung over the water, making the pathway narrow. The vertiginous drops and panoramic sea views were impressive and they couldn't resist stopping for photos.

"Damn! Look at all this graffiti," Stevie exclaimed. "And those bloody padlocks on the fences! I know I'm not a fan of romance at the moment, but I've never gotten on board with the so-called love locks."

"I dislike them too. Those blasted locks simply do damage. How is that romantic?" Kim complained.

Stephanie rolled her eyes. "Good question. Oh, to be back here a few hundred years ago when this path was first carved out of the steep hillside. Walking along here to meet your true love ... now that would have been romantic."

When they arrived at the kissing seat that was backed by a metal silhouette of two people locked in an embrace, they decided to get silly. Sitting on the seat together, they took several selfies as they laughed uproariously.

"Who has a better time than we do?" Kim asked. Stephanie's laugh ended with a snort which made them laugh even harder.

But in spite of their good time, Stephanie did find herself fighting back thoughts of how it might feel to share this breathtaking scenery with a special man who loved her. She squeezed her eyes shut and shook her head, banishing the image of Max that drifted into her fantasy.

When they reached the end of the trail at the village of Manarola, they found the family-run bistro Martha had recommended. They settled on a quiet terrace shaded by grape-laden vines on a pergola. Their delicious lunch consisted of homestyle grilled sardines and fresh pasta, followed by a heavenly tiramisù.

Feeling rested and eager to get going, they consulted their map. After a short walk out of town, they tackled a much more difficult trail. This one reached the highest point of the Cinque Terre hills. Steep steps offered the occasional challenge but lush vineyards and stunning views were the rewards. Try as they might, they could not make friends with several adorable-looking feral cats lurking along the way.

"Thank goodness for digital photography," Kim said. "Between these views and those cats, I can't begin to imagine how many shots I've taken." Then her voice softened and she moaned, "I miss Frank. These guys are making me feel guilty for leaving him, even though I know he is being spoiled. He will be waddling by the time I pick him up next month."

Stephanie laughed, picturing Kim's roly-poly cat adding more girth to his cuddly frame. "With your sister looking after him, you know he is doing just fine."

"Too fine, I'm sure," Kim said, with a chuckle.

Hiking down proved more arduous than climbing up. Both women were exhausted when they stumbled off the tender and onto the Dream Maker.

The ship was buzzing with excited conversation as

people returning from different hikes compared their experiences.

"There's no question, Cinque Terre is another place to come back to and stay for a longer time," Stevie commented. Kim agreed wholeheartedly.

Dinner that evening paired the specialties of Cinque Terre with local wine. Chef Romano explained why there were anchovies with practically everything and the history of the bright green pesto sauce made with local basil.

Stephanie had pointed out to Kim the plant, which grew wild all through the hills.

Because Stevie was giving her full attention to the delicious dishes being served and was still tired from the hike, she forgot that she was avoiding Max. Suddenly she found herself looking into his deep green eyes. Startled to discover him at their table, greeting the other seven diners, she put her hands on her cheeks which she felt beginning to burn.

As he chatted with each person, Max's eyes flitted to Stephanie's face with a look of recognition. She averted hers. Kim kicked Stephanie's leg under the table, knowing full well she was about to bolt. But Max had already reached her; there was no escape.

"*Allora, turista*, we meet again. But you are sitting down, so I feel safe." Max said.

Stevie met his gaze. Her voice was strong. "I'm very sorry I spilled your wine all over you the other evening.

Truly! It definitely was my fault—and I did apologize—but you didn't seem interested in hearing it then."

All eyes were on Stephanie as Max flashed her a captivating smile. She was shocked to feel attracted to him, when she was prepared to seriously dislike the guy. *No, no, no! He was a total jerk the other night. I'm not going to let that go just because he has gorgeous eyes and a killer way of using them.*

Chapter 19

The Apology

Stephanie took a deep breath. She told herself there was no point in acting like a silly school girl. She could handle this.

Max broke the silence. "You are right. I was not very kind —it was, after all, my favorite sports jacket—*non importa*! It cleaned up perfectly. *Sono desolata*. I apologize for my bad manners. I was really out of sorts because a rowdy group of tourists nearby had been driving us crazy. They were ejected from the patio just before you came along. We have a terrible situation in Portofino with too many tourists and I took my anger out on you. That's really not my style."

"*Sono desolata*. I'm sorry too." Stephanie said, the words slipping from her lips before she could stop them. She gulped and thought about how she was going to fix that.

"Ah, *tu parli italiano!*" Max looked startled.

"Well, just high school b-basic stuff," Stephanie stammered. Kim kicked her again and Stephanie dared not look at her.

Chef Romano called to Max from across the room.

"Got to go," Max said, taking in everyone at the table with his warm smile. "I hope you loved our menu this evening. We have all sorts of delicious surprises for you in the coming week. *Buona serata!* Enjoy your evening."

He shot Stephanie a quick look which she absolutely did not miss as her eyes were glued to him. She felt her face flush again as she looked away.

Everyone at the table spoke at once, asking about the mishap in Portofino and teasing her about the way Max looked at her. They all appeared to be aged between thirty and fifty, too old, Stevie thought, to be the person who was texting her about TikTok. She decided that it must be one of the younger crew members. This helped her to relax and enjoy their company.

As quickly as she could, Stephanie changed the subject. There were a few faces new to her at the table and she was curious about their stories. She was fascinated to learn that some of the crew had been with the cruise company for many years and considered their jobs to be long-term careers.

Word was that the evening entertainment in the crew quarters was card games. Kim told Stephanie that she had enjoyed being part of a serious bridge group on the previous cruise and was going to play two nights a week.

"No problem," Stephanie said. "As you know, I never did learn the game. Have fun. I found some excellent websites about local food, with recipes, and I can't wait to learn more. Because the Cinque Terre area was cut off for so many centuries, it has many unique specialities, which is so cool. The family kitchen was the testing ground."

Kim smiled. "You've always gotten more excited reading about recipes than anyone I've ever come across. Go for it! See you later."

Rather than go to their room, Stephanie found a sheltered spot on deck and settled into a comfortable lounge chair. The ship was moving slowly down the coast into more open water as it sailed towards Sorrento and the Amalfi coast.

Although she was engrossed in the recipes she was reading, her thoughts slipped away from time to time to Martha's words about turning thirty. When she set aside the pain of her break up, Stephanie could see that she had settled into a routine with Benny that had been more confining than she realized at the time.

Maybe she needed to open herself up to life in a more positive way. Certainly these first two weeks on the cruise were a great beginning. She had seen more landscapes and been exposed to more history than she had since her year at cooking school, which was almost eight years ago she suddenly realized.

How that time had slipped by. Benny hated flying, so all of their travel had been road trips, even right across Canada to the west coast. But any thoughts of Europe had been written off.

Now she kicked herself and vowed to make up for lost time.

CHAPTER 20

POSITANO, CAPRI AND THE AMALFI COAST

As it turned out, a good opportunity presented itself the next day.

The cruise itinerary called for a stop for one night in Sorrento before the ship moved on. It would then anchor off Positano, which Kim explained offered many more opportunities to explore achingly beautiful towns and the fabled Isle of Capri.

During a quiet moment in the afternoon at the boutique, the Roaring Forties—a group of four uproarious British women—dropped by, which meant goodbye to the quiet. The women were serious foodies from London who had introduced themselves at the jewelry boutique at the beginning of the cruise. Their fortieth birthdays were on the horizon and the cruise was a joint celebration.

"We're all into jewelry and want to buy something on the trip to celebrate the turn of the sun into our fifth decade," Lisa One had said early on. In the meantime, they had narrowed down their choices but were still trying to make a decision.

She was Lisa One to be distinguished from Lisa Two. Both were married and together they owned a trendy café in the Notting Hill area of London. Then there was Liz, a graphic designer, recently divorced, and Liane, devoted to her partner, Marie, with whom she owned a pet daycare business. Like Kim and Stephanie, they had known each other since childhood.

As had become their habit, they were sipping cocktails while they browsed.

"Have you ladies met the American group who are here celebrating their sixtieth birthdays?" Kim asked. "You should definitely crack a bottle or two of champagne together!"

They all admired Stephanie's epidote pendant. "You had sold out all of your pieces by the time we stopped by the day you were selling them. We were so disappointed," Liz said.

"I'm having more pieces with epidotes delivered from Toronto," Kim said. "I believe the shipment is being delivered later this afternoon, so I can get everything organized while you are all off for dinner this evening.

The women cheered. "We definitely want to see those," Liane said.

"When you wake up in Positano in the morning, Stephanie and I should have everything ready to display."

"Speaking of waking up in Positano, tomorrow we're renting a six-seater luxury van with a smart, sexy guide —" Lisa Two began, but was interrupted by Lisa One.

"Liz insisted the 'sexy' was the important part," Lisa One clarified, as they all laughed.

"Anyhoo, as I was saying," Lisa Two continued, "the plan is to drive along the coast to Pompei for the morning and then up to Ravello for a late lunch. We would love it if you joined us," they invited.

Kim looked at Stephanie and said, "You should go with them. I did that tour on the last cruise and Pompei is not to be missed."

Stephanie hesitated and Kim continued. "I can use the day to do more beading. We can organize the other jewelry later. No worries."

The next day, before sunrise, Kim roused Stephanie. "Come over to the window. I want you to see this. Liam told me last night what time we would be passing them, so I set my alarm."

Stephanie looked out at the sharp outlines of three tall, jagged rocks rising up from the sea and bathed in moonlight, "I Faraglioni," she sighed. "You were looking at them when you FaceTimed me about joining you. What a fateful day that was!"

"I figured you wouldn't mind getting up for this," Kim said.

"I would have hated to miss them. I mean— even the Greeks wrote about them. I know we will see them in daylight, but this is too good," Stevie said, as she grabbed her camera and popped off several shots. "The moonlight on them is amazing."

She pressed the button on the espresso machine. "I'm going to stay up and get some shots of Positano now and at sunrise."

"Okay," Kim said. "I'm going back to sleep for a couple of hours. The first day docking off Positano is always slow on the ship. Everyone wants to get off and explore. You are going to love it here."

Chapter 21

Pompei and Amalfi

As dawn was washing over the pastel-hues of the town of Positano, Stephanie and the Roaring Forties were dropped at the dock by the first tender from the ship.

"Every port is so spectacular on this trip," Liane gasped, her eyes glued to the scenery. The others murmured their agreement.

Lush green hills served as a backdrop for the town's pale pink, yellow and white buildings, all stacked in a vertical panorama that rose up from the turquoise sea. Beyond a wide beach, Stevie could see inviting terraces shaded by vibrant bougainvillea and multicolored umbrellas.

"Just imagine how many stairs one has to climb to get from street to street," Liane said. "It's exhausting just thinking about it."

Alberto, the swoon-worthy guide and chauffeur for the day, was parked just a few feet away along the dock. He introduced himself with exquisite manners to each woman before opening the door of the luxury Mercedes Sprinter van.

"Wowee! VIP all the way!" Liz Two exclaimed, as she climbed on.

"*Assolutamente*," Alberto replied. "Nothing but the best for you beautiful ladies today. You have only to ask."

That promise put broad smiles on all their faces as the women settled into the van's comfortable seats, each already supplied with water and a crescent-shaped cornetto on its armrest.

Alberto passed around an iPad showing the route he had planned, and said he hoped their early departure would mean the traffic would not be too bad. "It's a big problem here, with our narrow winding roads and spectacular scenery. The police are going to begin using some very strict rules about special days for cars to travel. But no worries today because you have me. And nothing is a problem for Alberto. *Andiamo*!" He flashed a dazzling smile, and Stevie was as beguiled as the others.

After explaining the trip would not take more than an hour, Alberto suggested they stop at a *benzinaio* for an espresso.

"Isn't that a gas station?" Lisa Two asked.

"Si!" Alberto said. "They have some of the best espresso bars in Italy."

A few minutes later, they were standing at a busy counter drinking espresso. He was right, they all agreed, the espresso was particularly good, and the busyness around them was entertaining. Adults were filling shopping carts with pasta, salami, wine and olive oil. Children were tossing in sweets and books. Waiters were taking orders in the restaurant and the crowd around the espresso bar was as lively as one in any posh neighbourhood. It was far from the gas- and petrol-station atmosphere the women were used to.

They made some purchases themselves and then climbed back into the van for the journey to the Archeological Park of Pompei. Mount Vesuvius loomed not so far away.

"It's hard to believe that such a peaceful looking part of the landscape left an entire city frozen in time over two thousand years ago," Alberto said.

Alberto was a certified guide for the park, and as they approached the ruins, he explained, "This was a rich Greco-Roman city until the eruption of Mount Vesuvius in 79 AD, and everything lay as it was covered under ash until it was unearthed in the early 1700s. We will see lavish villas, working-class homes, beautiful frescoes, even a brothel and, believe it or not, loaves of bread in an oven! It's quite remarkable."

He paused for a moment before adding, in a quiet tone, "There are also plaster casts of the bones of bodies as they fell or were caught in mid pose. So, I want to warn you that, in a way, Pompeii is also a cemetery."

From then on, the women spoke in hushed voices, expressing how they felt to be on hallowed ground. It was haunting to see bodies frozen in the middle of an action. Sharing comments non-stop, each one agreed that visiting this site was far more impressive than they had anticipated.

There was so much information to absorb and so many photos they wanted to take. Walking was difficult on the uneven ancient pathways and there were few opportunities to sit to rest.

"Ladies, I urge you to try and be present with what you are seeing. Don't lose yourself in setting up photos. You will miss the solemn immediacy of your experience. I will give you lists of websites where you can find books and photos of everything and explanations in more detail than you could possibly hear on a three-hour visit. And, *certamente*, there is a well-stocked gift shop."

They listened and nodded.

"You are right, Alberto. We're trying to record everything instead of really absorbing what is in front of us," Liz agreed. "It's amazing how much has been preserved through the thousands of years."

"Many people come and try to capture all the history here in one visit," Alberto said. "*E impossibile*. It's impossible."

Whenever Alberto was catching his breath or walking them to the next exhibit, the women talked among themselves about how they might have been captured by the eruption. The somber and fascinating surroundings wrapped around them.

Three hours under the blazing sun was more than enough for all of them, even though they had all brought water with them, and when Alberto suggested they move on to Ravello, they were happy to accept.

⚓

After a stop in the gift shop, they got back into the van and discovered a surprise waiting at each comfortable seat.

"Since you are going to enjoy lunch at a spectacular restaurant, we have provided a small antipasto in the van and refreshing mineral water. We don't want to spoil your appetite," Alberto said.

As they drove, the scenery kept everyone gasping. Alberto made several stops at lookouts, so they could take in the spectacular view. He pointed out the olive, lemon and chestnut groves and the abundance of rosemary growing wild in the hills. His knowledge of the history of the area brought to life the laborious efforts through the centuries to build and work the terraced vineyards and groves that climbed the steep hills.

"I show you all this so you know where to go the next time you come," Alberto said, as he drove, his voice extra sultry. "Because you will return to Amalfi—everyone does!"

Lisa One and Two fanned themselves with their hands behind his back. Liane rolled her eyes and nodded in agreement. Liz feigned fainting.

Stephanie chuckled. She was starting to realize she had cut herself off from having fun with other women. When she wasn't knocking herself out at the trattoria, she was doing something with Benny, or reading about cooking, or sleeping. And then there was the pandemic. Now she was enjoying being herself with four interesting women who knew how to make the most of life and savor the small moments.

She was not paying much attention to where they

were when Alberto announced they were nearing Ravello, their next destination. Then he turned the van off the coastal road, and drove them up a road with the most switchbacks that Stephanie had ever been on. All the women clutched their armrests and held their breaths as the Mercedes climbed 350 meters from sea level to the top. "This is Ravello," Alberto announced, sweeping his arm. "I will show you the town, *ma prima mangiamo*. But first we eat." He parked in the lot of a small café with an enormous terrace hanging over the cliffs that swept down to the sea.

Tables with white linen cloths and elegant china and crystal had been set up under a grape-laden pergola. The view down and along the sun-washed coast was heart stopping.

"Hello vertigo!" Liz called out as the others nodded their agreement and gulped their replies.

The maitre'd greeted them with "*Benvenuti*" in a melodic voice, and escorted them to the table with absolutely the best view.

Lisa One looked at Alberto. "I thought we'd chosen a pizza place for lunch. Not that I'm disappointed, just confused."

"*Si! É questo!* This is it!" Alberto said, as the women looked on in amused disbelief. "You said you just wanted pizza for lunch because you will have a feast tonight on the ship. *Ecco qua!* Here you are—the best pizza place *and* the best view! Did I do a good job?" Everyone laughed and applauded.

Once they were seated, waiters appeared with five delicious-looking pizzas and small carafes of wine. The head waiter, who wore a white shirt, black pants and a long black apron tucked at his waist, explained how each pizza was different. He also gave them a detailed description of the local wine they were being served. They were offered other options if the chosen one did not please them. No one complained.

Lisa Two was fanning herself this time. "How is it that everything said by a man with an Italian accent sounds soooo sexy and impossible to resist?"

Alberto had discreetly disappeared while they were served and after the waiters left, the conversation turned to the subject of Italian men. There was a quiet debate about Alberto's age, which they guessed was mid-thirties. They agreed that his thoughtfulness, good humor, and his knowledge were all more than they could have hoped for.

"And he hits the sexy factor out of the park," Liz said. "I'm having hot flashes and it's not from menopause, I assure you. I can't keep my eyes off him and as soon as he speaks, I'm in rapture."

At one point, Stephanie said, "Well, my Italian man became less sexy and impossible to resist as time went by —but then he didn't have the accent."

"That's the key. The accent," Liz said, after expressing sympathy for Stephanie and her break up. All the women offered their commiseration.

"Thanks," Stephanie responded, "I'm pretty much over it. This cruise was just the ticket. Kim always has the best ideas and the timing could not have been better."

Conversation moved on after a few minutes of comparing past breakups.

"Hey, it's part of what happens, right? And we move on. You sound like you are feeling that now Stephanie."

"For sure," Stephanie said, rubbing the stone of her epidote pendant, "I'm still not sure where I'm going, but I'll get there."

Admiring the necklace, Liane asked, "So have you found that stone is bringing you good vibes? Is it energizing your chakra?"

"I'm working on it," Stephanie said with a smile.

"I can't wait until Kim gets some more of her supply in. She said it was coming this afternoon, right? I want to buy something like that for Marie."

The two Lisas were deep in an inspection of their pizzas. "There's something so different about the dough compared to what we make at the café," Lisa One said.

Lisa Two agreed. "The texture is so light with just the right amount of crispiness on this slightly charred outside and light and airy on the inside."

"And—mmm—what is that subtle flavor?" Lisa One asked.

Stephanie could not help joining in. She knew precisely what they meant and she felt herself fill with pleasure as she spoke. Her eyes sparkled. "Well, ladies. We are eating the unique Unesco recognized *verra pizza Napolitana*—Neapolitan pizza. Specific rules from the eighteenth century must be followed for the dough. No rolling pins or mechanical presses allowed. It needs two stages of proofing, with a final proof of least eight hours. Then it's baked in a wood-fired oven at eight to nine hundred degrees Fahrenheit for only sixty to ninety seconds."

She paused for a moment and then added, "It's the most digestible pizza dough in the world because of the little bubbles in it caused by that process."

Then she bit her lip and looked down at the table. "Sorry for going on. I couldn't help myself!"

The four women stared at her. "Well, you're certainly well informed," Liz said with a chuckle. The others nodded. "And thank you for telling us. That's so cool. I've heard Naples referred to as the home of pizza but never really knew why."

Stephanie felt her cheeks flush. She had not meant to blather on about it.

The women stared at her for a moment and then Lisa One said, "Stephanie, don't be cross with us. We know who you are."

"StevieV's Pasta Party!" Lisa Two said, her voice filled with affection. "Lisa and I have followed you for years on TikTok."

They both broke into the quirky hand jive routine Stephanie did at the end of each video.

"After all, we are in the food business too, and we are total fangirls of yours. You're amazing!"

Lisa One joined in. "Kim asked us not to say anything when we asked her about you. But how can we not now that we're not hiding anything?"

Stephanie stammered, "Well—well—um—Kim probably told you I didn't want anyone on the ship to know."

Liz said, "Well someone does know. It's kind of all over social media, and none of us has said a thing."

Stephanie looked shocked. "I've been off all social media for weeks now."

"Somebody started a Facebook page called Where in the World is Stevie Valentini?—you know, like the video game Where in the World is Carmen Sandiego?" Liane said. "And people are speculating about where you are."

"But it's all in good fun. Don't worry!" Liane said.

"Someone on the ship knows where you are, but they're not saying. They just drop hints every now and then on the page saying you were in Italy, but they don't say how you got there," Liz added.

Stephanie felt deeply embarrassed and remained quiet.

Lisa One reached out for her hand. "Hey! We are thrilled to know you for you, so please don't be embarrassed. We won't breathe a word. But feel free to share your food expertise with us any time. You know we are foodies too, and there's nothing we like talking about more."

"Well, some of us like talking about men more," Liz said. Everyone laughed, which cleared the air.

"Thanks," Stephanie said. "I guess I was a bit stupid to think I could keep things a secret. I'm just trying to sort out my life and stop thinking about food and cooking Italian twenty-four-seven—because that's kind of what I do. In fact, I think that's what broke up my relationship with Benny—my one-track mind."

Lisa Two said, "Don't beat yourself up about that. You're lucky you have such a passion in your life. I'm sure you will fall in love again."

Stephanie waved her hands, brushing the thought

away with a grimace. "One thing about this trip that I do not want is any romantic involvement. *Nessuno!*"

"Yeah, yeah! We will see about that. It's hard to avoid on a cruise," Liz said. "Although we chose this one because we figured there would not be a lot of eligible men in our age range and that's what we wanted. No romantic interference! This is a girls' trip, period!"

"Although part of a girls' trip is talking about men," Lisa Two said, "even when we are happily married."

To that they all, including Stephanie, raised their glasses. Over the last of the wine they agreed they were not going to talk about how Pompei affected them until dinner.

"Too serious a conversation for this setting," Liane said.

A waiter approached them. He set down a plate of light and flaky Italian cookies and poured them each a small glass of local limoncello.

Alberto magically reappeared seconds after they had finished to suggest they leave for their tour of two medieval villas as soon as they were ready. Liz was first out of her chair.

Ravello was as stunning as they had been told, with tree-lined avenues, flourishing gardens, and ancient villas. It called to be explored.

Two hours later, after touring the elegant palazzi and two secluded villas, all with extensive lush gardens, Alberto headed the van down the winding road. "Now we go to Amalfi for gelato, si?"

A robust response of "Si!" filled the van.

"*É cos oltro*? What else in Amalfi?" Alberto asked.

"Shoes!" the women all chorused. The town's hand-made, custom-fitted fine leather shoes and sandals were legendary.

Alberto mentioned the name of one shop and there was a collective shriek. The women had done their homework.

Liz moved up near the front of the van and chatted with Alberto about the shoe store and then the scenery they were passing. She was enthralled.

In the town of Amalfi, they strolled along picturesque narrow medieval streets to the main square in front of the Duomo. They stopped there to refresh themselves with servings of gelato, and Alberto encouraged them to refill their water bottles from the famous marble Fontana sant'Andrea, where clear drinkable water spouted from the nipples of the ample bosoms of the baroque statuary.

The streets were becoming busy with families strolling and Alberto explained that this was the beginning of the daily *passeggiata*, a longstanding pre-dinner tradition in all Italian towns.

"Everyone comes out for a late afternoon, early evening stroll to greet each other and feel a sense of community," he said. "We will join them for a while, if you wish."

"That was one of my favorite parts of living in Italy," Stephanie told them, happy to be able to share that now they knew who she was.

For half an hour they sauntered and returned greetings of *buona sera* with smiling strangers.

Then they were off in search of new footwear.

CHAPTER 22

AMALFI COAST FEAST

Once all their parcels were loaded in Alberto's van, they were on their way back to the ship as the sun was beginning to slip to the horizon.

There were friendly nudges in the back as Liz was sitting in the passenger seat next to Alberto. They had begun chatting as the group walked back to the van and she was now engrossed in conversation with him.

Alberto continued to make occasional stops so they could admire the striking countryside and vast panoramic view along the coast. At times, he pulled over where there did not seem to be anything in particular to see and then would direct them to look straight down. At the foot of a sheer cliff, there would be a gem of a beach dotted with colorful umbrellas and with boats bobbing in the water nearby.

"Many of our beaches are best reached by boat," he told them. "Or else you have to climb up and down hundreds of steps! But whatever way you go it is worth it.

There is something about the sea along the Amalfi coast that feels magical."

When they arrived at the dock, having texted for the next tender arrival time, Alberto issued an invitation. "My cousin has a boat and I have just been talking to him. We would like to invite you all to go out with us tomorrow as our guests. It is a day off for both of us and you are such good company. Think about it and let me know this evening."

They assured him they would soon be in touch and cheerfully replied to his "*Arrivederci!*"

By the time they reached the Dream Maker, they had made their decision. Stephanie had declined but encouraged the others to go. "I've got work to do on the ship but you should definitely accept the invitation. What a wonderful opportunity!"

They headed to their cabins, calling out "See you at dinner!"

When Stephanie opened the door to the cabin all she could see was an immense floral arrangement consisting of every color of rose imaginable. Their sweet fragrance filled the room.

Kim spread her arms toward it and announced, "Ta da! For you!"

"For heaven's sake! Really?" Stephanie picked the card out of the blossoms. It read: "*Ti prego perdonami.* Please forgive me. Max."

She sat down and stared at the beauty in front of her. "Wow! I guess he means it."

Kim nodded. "Perhaps you should try being nice to him now."

Dinner that evening was a feast featuring local, Amalfi offerings. Lemon was the star. Stephanie found her taste buds coming alive in a way she had feared was lost to her.

She was glad she and Kim were seated at a table for two this evening so she could fill her in on the events of the day. There was only one thing missing now. Max was nowhere to be seen and Stephanie could not stop herself from watching for him.

The meal began with the grandest display of antipasto Stephanie had ever laid eyes on, including a section devoted to *crudo misto,* raw seafood, with oysters, fish carpaccio, anchovies in oil, and raw red shrimp.

Primi piatti offered the most divine pastas. Among the choices were ravioli filled with ricotta and lemon zest and spaghetti with *coloratura*, the famous Amalfi sauce made with the anchovies from the tiny village of Cetara. Renowned throughout the world, fishermen here use the same method from ancient Etruscan times.

Chef Romano made a point of saying this was THE dish of the Amalfi coast.

Secondi piatti, brought out beef, chicken, and fish served with salads and a variety of *contorni*.

Stephanie looked at Kim and crossed her eyes. "I've already reached my limit tonight. But Chef Romano is definitely reawakening my joy for this kind of food."

Kim laughed. "I know you. Dessert is still to come. But I am so happy to hear you talk about cooking again. You've been so silent, I was getting worried."

"This afternoon with the Roaring Forties kind of

kicked me over the edge again. I couldn't resist opening up. And they made me feel good about it."

A dessert extravaganza was rolled out on an over-loaded trolley.

"Oh please!" Kim wailed. "How can I resist something called *Delizia al Limone*. You've been keeping secrets, Stevie. I don't recall you ever mentioning this dessert."

Stephanie explained the dessert was a Genoise sponge cake soaked in limoncello syrup, filled with lemon-based cream, and covered with lemon cream glaze.

"The last time I saw one of those was at school in Florence. You, being the lemon-lover you are, will adore it!" Stephanie said. "I love it too. But I also love this flourless chocolate Caprese cake. It should be crunchy on the outside, sensuously soft inside. I think that's what I'll have."

Along with several other pastries, there was a variety of flavors of gelato and granita on offer, but Stephanie and Kim stuck with their choice of cakes, and both declared them absolute perfection.

Everyone was served a glass of limoncello to top off the meal in the best Amalfi fashion and the room cheered as Chef Romano took a bow. Max had still not appeared.

Stephanie leaned over to Kim, hoping to look nonchalant. "Did anyone mention that Max was going to be away this evening?"

Kim shook her head. "But I did notice you scanning the room through the entire meal."

Stephanie shrugged. "Just thought I should say thank you for the flowers."

Kim snorted.

They were about to leave when the Roaring Forties arrived at their table in their usual flamboyant fashion. "Come and have a nightcap with us!"

Once they all settled into the bar, there was non-stop conversation about the day they had shared. They were all emotional about the Pompei visit.

"We were so excited in the afternoon while visiting beautiful Ravello and shopping in Amalfi, we really did not stop to truly consider our visit to Pompei and all we experienced there," Liz said

"So haunting," Laurie murmured. To which everyone agreed. They shared some photos now as well.

"It was an amazing day! We were so lucky to have Alberto as our guide," Lisa One said. "Right, Liz?"

The last two words were added with a chuckle and a wink of her eye.

"Well, yes." Liz told Stephanie and Kim. "Okay—don't judge me."

"Absolutely not," Stephanie replied. "He seemed like a very kind, decent guy and—okay—definitely sexy."

Liz gave her a squinty eye look.

"Just kidding!" Stephanie said. "It's all cool."

Liz continued, "Alberto and I seem to have struck a chord. We've been texting all evening. He is picking the four of us up in the morning at the dock in his cousin's boat and they are going to tour us around for the day. He invited you too, Steph."

"Thanks! But as I mentioned, we have a busy few days in the boutique now with Kim's wonderful new pieces. But we can't wait to hear all about it!"

As they walked back to their cabin, Kim said, "You see, you never know what's going to happen on a vacation. Tomorrow will be a day they will never forget."

"Well," Stephanie said, "I will never forget today. It was amazing—right up until dessert tonight! There was only one thing missing."

"And what was that," Kim asked.

"Where was Max?" Stephanie mused.

"I thought you said he was jerk," Kim teased.

Stephanie shrugged. "I told you I just need to say thank you."

CHAPTER 23

CHEF ROMANO

Stephanie and Kim spent the next morning taking inventory in the shop. They had almost finished when they were surprised by a visit from Chef Romano himself.

"*Buongiorno signore*. May I invite you for a coffee?" he asked, addressing both women, a warm smile creasing his expressive face. Stephanie wondered if she had ever seen such a handsome—and seemingly unaware of it —older man.

"*Buongiorno* Chef Romano," she replied, wide-eyed. She bowed her head to him. "*Che onore vederti*. What an honor to see you here."

Kim extended her hand. "Chef Romano! What a pleasant surprise."

"I have a day off and was hoping you might have some time for a chat," the chef said.

Stephanie still appeared flabbergasted but Kim calmly said, "How lovely of you. Thank you."

"*Buoni*," he said, with another smile. "I took the

liberty of arranging for us to have some espresso privately served in the library."

As they followed him into the cozy, book-lined room, Kim gently poked Stephanie, who got the message.

The relaxing ambiance of the room was enhanced by the aroma of strong espresso filling the air. Miniature marizotti, biscotti and cornetti were temptingly arranged on a platter.

The three looked at each other for a moment before the chef broke the silence. "So, Stephanie Valentini, we meet at last—and not for the first time! And please introduce me to your charming friend—although I have already heard fine words about her presence on the ship."

Stephanie was taken aback by his saying that this was not their first meeting. She swallowed to compose herself. He—one of her culinary heroes—was sitting inches from her, wanting a conversation. She could do this.

"Of course, Chef. This is such an honour. Please may I introduce my closest friend, Kimberly Lake."

Romano reached out once more to shake Kim's hand, looking deeply into her eyes with a gaze of pure friendship. Then he reached for Stephanie's hand and clasped it in both of his.

"*Signorina Stephanie, sa che siamo una famiglia*? We are family, you know."

Stephanie felt like an idiot as she stammered," M-my Nonna Bella s-said ..."

Romano squeezed her hands, still clasped in his. "Your Nonna Bella emailed me when I first came on the ship and we have had two FaceTime chats since—*Figurati*! Imagine! After so many years."

Stephanie still could not speak and hoped her mouth was not hanging open. She was in shock.

He continued, "One thing about Italians—when you are family, you are family forever. Because our ancestors emigrated all over the world, we often lose touch but we never stop being family."

Stephanie nodded and finally found her voice. "My family has always stressed that. We have a plaque in our foyer that says *Chi si volta, e chi si gira, sempre a casa va finire.* I know it means wherever you go or turn, you will always end up at home.' And my Nonna always said it's because Italian homes are always there for family."

"She's a wise woman. And right." Romano agreed.

Stephanie shook her head, still amazed. "But how did you and I meet?"

He laughed – a soft, tender sound, in spite of his robust size. "You and I met when you came over to Marzabotta with your Nonna and Bisnonna and parents. My grandmother was also from Paola's village and one of the survivors—her cousin. She had a big reunion during your visit, which you might not remember. You were maybe ten and I was in my fifties with children your age. I remember you all played together. There must have been a hundred people at the gathering. What a celebration!"

Stephanie felt herself relaxing now, faintly sensing a family connection in spite of the years. What was it? she wondered. She rubbed her tattoo and felt a warm rush.

"I do remember an enormous party in a village square, and we kids were running everywhere. My parents have photos from that day. Wow, so you were there—and your family ..."

They all sat sipping their espresso for a moment, processing all that had just been shared.

"But how did Nonna Bella connect with you now? Have you always been in touch?" Stevie asked.

"Oh no! But the women have kept communication open. At first, they wrote letters. Somehow, they always know where family is, even extended family. When Paola left, there were only two other cousins who survived—*il massacor ...la tragedia ...*" He quickly crossed himself, saying, "*Grazie a Dio*. And their families never forgot. Just like your Bisnonna."

"I did not realize the connection remained, which makes me feel very badly now," Stephanie said. "But I'm so thankful Nonna Bella contacted you."

"Si! It was a great surprise. And then to learn you were on this ship. We have had such fine chats. I know all about your success in the kitchen—that you possess the family *all'italiana* cooking genes, the magic. How you have saved Cara Mia during this shocking—*la pandemia*. It has been so, so hard on Italy."

Stephanie began to protest but he gently shushed her with his hands and a knowing look. "And my nephew Maximus has told me he knows you from this TikaToka —StevieV's Pasta Party. *Cosi brillante*. He showed me."

Stephanie blushed, feeling completely embarrassed. "Very juvenile compared to your fine cuisine."

"No! *No è quest il punto*. That's not the point. It's all about feeling, loving, sensing the cooking of Italian—and you have that. You share that. Maximus has followed you for years."

Stephanie gasped in disbelief.

"So are they cousins too?" Kim asked.

"Ah, no—Maximus is my nephew from my wife's side of the family. But still—we really are all one big family in every other way."

Kim blew a barely noticeable sigh of relief then politely excused herself, saying that they didn't need her around for family chat. Romano kissed her fingers as she stood up, then turned back to Stephanie.

"Stephanie, today is a special day for me. Captain Keeling always plans this. We go by helicopter to Ravello and dine at the most exclusive, but simple, Italian kitchen. Then we return to the ship and rest, and tonight I am the guest of honor at the Michelin-star restaurant the passengers will visit. Will you come along as my guest?"

"Oh Chef Romano ..." she began.

"Please call me Emilio, we are family," he said.

"Emilio, this is such an honor. Such a surprise. I am so happy. But honestly, I do not feel it is right for me to go along on this special day for you. I hope you understand." Stephanie hoped she did not sound ungrateful.

With a sincere expression, Emilio took her hand. "*Si, capisco*. I wish I could change your mind. But I understand. I'm sure this is all quite a shock to you—but a good one. We have a few more days together on the ship and in Sicily before I leave. Will you promise to spend some time in the kitchen with me here? One day we go together for a special visit in Sicily—we have family there too!"

Stephanie nodded in agreement, and Emilio stood to

go, then asked if he could hug her—saying yet again "*Famiglia—siempre famiglia* ...".

Her nod allowed him to gently envelop her in his massive embrace.

Stephanie immediately walked back to the cabin, passing Kim in the boutique on the way and gesturing for her to follow. She flopped on her bed, feeling emotionally exhausted and Kim walked in a few seconds later.

They looked at each other and squealed. "Can you believe it?" Kim asked. "Can you flippin' believe it? Damn! I wish I was Italian!"

Stephanie stared at the ceiling and finally said, "Paola knew this was going to happen, and bless Nonna Bella for making it so. My tattoo is burning. Seriously. Feel this."

Kim did and was surprised how hot it was. "That's astonishing!" she said. Then she added with a mischievous grin, "So you are related to the renowned Chef Romano, but not at all to his nephew Max. How about that!"

CHAPTER 24

ARRIVEDERCI, AMALFI COAST

Stephanie and Kim spent the afternoon unpacking the beadwork that had arrived on board. Then they reorganized the displays. Stephanie could not stop exclaiming at the new pieces as she unwrapped each one.

"Kim, you grabbed all the amazing colors of the Amalfi coast to make these stunning pieces. Vibrant yellows, brilliant blues and greens, with touches of so many different shades. These will sell fast."

Martha dropped by later on, looking exhausted.

"I couldn't wait to see your new pieces, Kim," she said.

Kim showed her a few pieces she thought Martha would most like.

"They are stunning!" Martha said. She chose two to set aside.

"Ladies, I understand, but I'm sorry you could not fit in the hike I just finished. You would have loved it. Make a plan for when you return, because—as everyone assures us here—you will return." She chuckled. "For someone who has been here as many times as I have, I know they are right."

"You did the Path of the Gods, right?" Stephanie asked.

"Yes. Not the most difficult hike, but still lots of stairs and some narrow paths around cliffs. But the most spectacular scenery ever. Seriously! And now it's time for a nap!"

"I love her energy," Stephanie said, watching Martha disappear down the corridor.

"Speaking of energy," Kim said, "Lisa One just texted to see if we would join them to swim for a couple of hours off Alberto's cousin's boat. Apparently, they can pick us up right here at the ship, if we can be ready by three."

"Let's do it!" Stephanie said.

Alberto's cousin Matteo was another charmer and his "boat" was more like a yacht. The twenty people on it did not seem like a crowd at all. Their ages ranged from teenagers to Matteo's parents in their seventies. His mother was in the kitchen cheerily preparing food with help from time to time from assorted guests, including the Roaring Forties. Stevie said to Kim later, it felt like a family gathering.

His father was driving the boat and Matteo said that he was leaving it to him to choose the best anchoring spots.

Stephanie and Kim were greeted most hospitably by

everyone. The two Lisas and Liane couldn't stop describing the marvellous day they were having. "Mamma has even taught us how to put together some amazing antipasto!"

Liz and Alberto appeared to be spending most of their time together, although they did make a point of greeting Stephanie and Kim.

Conversation was non-stop accompanied by laughter and comments on every topic imaginable. Food and drink, much of it non-alcoholic lemonade and fruit seltzers, was served non-stop.

"*Famiglia*," Stephanie whispered to Kim. "Like Emilio said. It's the Italian way."

Everyone was enjoying the hot day and the refreshing turquoise water of the Tyrrhenian Sea. Swimming in the grottos was the main focus.

Stephanie and Kim soon joined others in the sea and were astonished when they followed some under rocky arches and through narrow openings at the bottom of cliffs. The light in the grottos was magical. As sunlight filtered through, it became tinged with fluorescent electric blue that sparkled as it reflected off the walls.

"I've never seen anything like this," Stephanie exclaimed, as Kim and others agreed.

As the sun began to set, bowls of salad, baskets of bread and platters of simple pastas were set out. Wine was poured and a quieter ambiance settled in before Matteo delivered the *Dream Maker* passengers back to the ship. Liz explained she had been invited to spend the night at the home of Alberto's parents and would join the ship before its departure time in the morning.

Grateful *grazies* filled the air.

Feeling as though they had eaten more than enough, Stephanie and Kim skipped going into the dining area. Instead they went to the outdoor terrace bar and were soon joined by Liam and Katherine, who were anxious to hear all about their day.

In time, others from the kitchen joined the group, including Maximus, who arrived with Jean-Marc and Nicole. Stephanie made a point of going to speak to him.

"*Grazie mille.* Thank you very much for the stunning flowers, along with your note. It was most thoughtful—and appreciated."

"*Di nulla,*" Max replied. He stood and pulled over an empty chair, as others moved to make room. With a grin he said, "Would you like to stay and chat for a while now we are on speaking terms?"

"For a while" turned into hours as the two discovered how similar their upbringings had been. How food and family were intertwined and love was the underlying factor. They agreed they shared the *all'italiana*, Italian style gene, which simply could not be denied.

"*Famiglia*—family is everything." he murmured,

"But not to the exclusion of anything else" Stephanie also murmured. "And that is what I'm being reminded of these past few weeks. Family encompasses so much and I had lost touch with that."

Their eyes met in a moment of understanding.

Stephanie felt a quiver of uncertainty as she became

aware of the warm feelings for Max she could not deny. It was all so unexpected.

By this time, the evening had turned to night, and the bright moon was reflecting off the sea. She noticed the way it caught the relaxed outline of his jaw and the slight parting of his lips.

"Now I know it's in our genes and cannot be denied," Max said. "It took me a while to come to terms with that. But for some time I have embraced the fact that everything about food—the learning, the cooking, the tasting, the serving to others—is an important part of who I am. I am lost without it."

Stephanie listened carefully to his words, recognizing they were also hers.

"The same is true for me. It's my passion," she said. "I read a quote once that said cooking is the new meditation."

"I've seen that too," Max replied. "It implied when we cook we create moments of pure happiness."

Stephanie nodded. "But along with that this time on the ship has reminded me that I want to travel, to experience everything life has to offer including cooking, and not be limited to one place all the time," Stephanie said.

Max nodded. "Zio Emilio suggested that you and I could join him in the kitchen tomorrow. Are you up for that?"

"Up for it? Yes! Intimidated? Also yes!" Then, not too effectively, she stifled a yawn. "Sorry. It's been quite the day."

Max laughed. "Allow me to walk you to your cabin.

Tomorrow is a long day at sea—lots of time to get creative in the kitchen!"

CHAPTER 25

SICILY BECKONS

The next day, Kim refused to consider Stephanie working in the boutique at all.

"Are you kidding me? It's a unique opportunity for you to cook with Chef Romano and Max. Go for it! I know I will be one of the recipients of your kitchen magic today."

The Chef had texted her to report to the galley at eight *in punto* for *magia culinaria*. "That's 8 a.m. sharp for culinary magic," she translated for Kim. "This will be quite the morning!"

When she arrived, on the dot of eight, Emilio and Max were both there. Emilio was wearing a white shirt, white pants, a white chef's hat, and a long white monogrammed apron he had plundered from the ship's stock. Max was similarly attired. They made a ceremony of handing Stephanie the same costume.

There was a blackboard on the counter with several dishes listed.

"But first, Stephanie, please begin with your *sugo—*

Paola's sauce," Chef Romano asked, almost reverently. "That is a must—if you will honor us. All the ingredients are here. But we know that anyone can make it with the same ingredients and it will not have the magic of yours. Because that is the secret. Not one ingredient—but the magic of you preparing it."

And so the entire day went, with each of them challenging the other. Max and Stephanie learned as they went—and Emilio often clapped in glee as he in turn learned something new from his young charges. They honed techniques, tweaked textures and flavors, suggested new ingredients and tried unique combinations. The dishes they crafted— some original and others old favourites with a new twist—all looked wonderful and tasted delicious.

The afternoon ended in hilarity when Max suggested they record some TikTok videos. Chef Romano proved to be a surprising entertainer. Encouraged by everyone, he got right into the singing, dancing and flipping pans and pasta. Many of the other staff joined in and much time was spent wiping away tears of laughter.

That evening, after dinner was finished, Emilio brought Max and Stephanie out to take a bow with him. A standing ovation was what they received.

Captain Keeling asked Stephanie if they could speak in the next few days about her playing a more active role in the kitchen for the remainder of the cruise. Then several bottles of the finest champagne were opened and emotional speeches were given. Stephanie was particularly touched by the depth of feeling when Chef

Romano and Captain Keeling spoke about their friendship, which spanned thirty years.

"*Famiglia* is what you hear me speak of incessantly when I speak of Italia," Emilio said. "I think one feels this most in our country—but I also feel it when I am on a ship like the *Dream Maker*. We all share a wonderful experience and we become *famiglia*. Thank you for allowing me to be part of yours during these past days."

Stephanie could feel a serious case of hiccups threatening and knew she had reached her limit with champagne.

"It's definitely time for me to get to bed," she said, excusing herself from the table. "Thank you to everyone for an unforgettable day."

Max stood and offered to walk back to the cabin with her. Kim had left the party earlier.

They talked and laughed easily on the way and when they reached her door, Max said softly, "May I ask you something?"

Stevie felt herself tense slightly. Is he going to kiss me? Why doesn't he just do it? Wait! Do I want him to?

Max looked down for a moment and then asked, "May I call you Stevie?" He had such a sincere expression, Stephanie wasn't certain if she wanted to laugh or cry.

"Of course!" she replied.

"I know it sounds a bit crazy but that's really how I know you. How I think of you! StevieV! I've been following you for years on TikTok. You're famous here in Italy and you don't even know it."

Stephanie blushed—and felt a little unsteady.

"Well, that's fine with me," she said.

Max leaned forward and kissed her lightly on each cheek. "If it is okay with you, may I pick you up at four tomorrow afternoon? There's something special I would like to show you."

Stevie's feet did not touch the floor as she walked into the cabin, shut the door and flopped on her bed.

"Whoa! Someone's got a very happy face." Kim said. Stevie nodded with a dreamy expression before she passed out. Kim removed her shoes and covered her with a light blanket.

CHAPTER 26

SICILY

The next morning, the passengers awoke to a view completely different from those of the past days. The *Dream Maker* was in the port of Messina, Sicily, tied up to a dock more or less on the main street, as opposed to the offshore anchorages they had experienced along the coast. The romantic, colorful scenes of the past ten days had changed dramatically.

Stevie went to the window for a good look. "Wow! How cool is this?" she exclaimed. "Those look like volcanic mountains right outside town and as far as I can see."

"Yup, that's what they are. The highest peak is Mount Etna, the only active volcano in Europe. Sicilians call her 'Mamma' because so much of their economy depends upon her. She rules their lives. Here endeth my lesson for the moment," Kim said. "Now hurry up and get ready. We are dashing out to eat *the best* cannoli ever!"

Liam and Katherine were waiting for them on the

quay and in minutes they had crossed the street and entered a bustling *pasticceria*. "Sicily is the true home of the cannoli!" Liam announced.

Lively chatter and the rich aroma of freshly roasted coffee filled the air. As they waited their turn in line, they watched tray upon tray of delectable pastries being brought out from the kitchen. Bare spots on the shelves were filled as quickly as they appeared. A few people behind the counter were singing. Then it was their turn to place their orders, and the cannoli were made for them right away.

"Can't get any fresher than this," Liam said after taking a bite. "This *Pasticceria* is always our first stop when we dock in Messina."

"Today's going to be a busy one for most passengers. Lots of day trips! We could spend a week in Sicily, easily. It's such a diverse culture and there's so much to see," Katherine said.

As they strolled back to the ship, Liam asked Kim, "So which hike did you finally decide to do here?"

"We are going with a small group tomorrow to do the six-hour sunset hike from Taormina to Etna. We decided it was best not to go on our own," Kim said.

"Wise choice—and decision. You will love it," Katherine said with Liam nodding in agreement. "Taormina is something special."

The afternoon passed quickly at the boutique.

From the beginning of the cruise, passengers knew that each time the ship docked Kim would offer a new selection of jewellery inspired by that location. Even though sales could not be completed until the ship was out to sea again, these layaway viewings had turned into popular party times too.

Martha was among the first to stop by. "Stephanie, congratulations on your day cooking with the Chef! The food was so delicious and different that evening. You must have had quite a memorable time."

Stephanie smiled modestly. "It was an incredible day. Thanks."

They asked Martha what she planned to do while they were in Messina, and it turned out she had a friend who lived in the town. "I'm going to be off ship a lot while we are here. It's a wonderful opportunity for my friend and me to catch up. How about you?"

While they were talking, Max texted. Stephanie felt a frisson of happiness that went all the way to her toes. It had been a long time since that had happened.

"I'll pick you up around 4 and I'll be on a motorcycle. If that's ok. If not, just let me know."

"Sounds great. I'll wear jeans," Stephanie texted back.

"Well," she said to Martha, suspecting her face betrayed her excitement, "It looks like I'll be having an adventure on a motorcycle later today."

"Wonderful! That sounds like something you should be doing!" Martha said, her eyes twinkling. "There's been a very happy air about you these past couple of days. I've remembered your great-grandmother's words, Steph. Perhaps she was right."

Stephanie grinned back, and touched her tattoo.

At 4:00 p.m. she was on the quay, standing beside the one street that gave access to the port. She was wearing jeans and was carrying a jean jacket in case she needed it later.

Minutes later Max pulled up on a gleaming black Benelli. He greeted Stephanie with a light kiss on each cheek and handed her a helmet.

"Are you cool with this, Stevie? I can rent a car if you prefer?" he asked.

"This is great! I'm up for an adventure," she assured him, feeling a little thrill run through her on hearing Max call her Stevie. It felt good. It felt right.

He helped her adjust her helmet and showed her how to use the audio so they could talk to each other.

Then he hopped on the bike and she climbed on behind him.

For a moment, fear stabbed her as she realized she had to wrap her arms around Max. This kind of physical contact with a man had become unfamiliar. A reminder of hurt. Was she ready to trust a man again? But as she slipped her arms around Max's waist, she realized she was more than ready.

After a short trip through the narrow streets of the oldest part of town, the road widened and followed the shimmering coastline even as it began to wind and climb.

As they entered a landscape of lemon and orange groves, almond orchards and vineyards, Max regaled her with the rich history of ancient Greeks and Romans in the area. Soon they were sharing more details of their own histories. They both knew they were connected through the tragic events in Marzabotta. Chef Romano had talked with them about what had happened there. He too carried the story in his soul.

But now their conversation became more current and personal. Stevie poured her heart out, describing how keeping Cara Mia alive through the pandemic had been her focus for two years, and how much she blamed herself for the failure of her relationship with Benny.

Max listened intently. Then he told her that he too once had to choose whether his true love was the kitchen or the kind of social life favored by his preppy girlfriend. The kitchen won.

"I decided the life of a party guy did not suit me," he said and then hastily added, "But don't get me wrong. I still like to have fun!"

Stevie's voice caught as she repeated the words her Bisnonna had left with her, *"Sei il custode della nostra magia di famiglia"*. "I'm supposed to carry on the family magic. She said if I went to Marzabotta, the spirit of Stefano would show me what I am to do."

"It's obvious she was a special woman," Max whispered. "Perhaps there is wisdom in her words."

"I often wonder," Stephanie said, "and I'm confused about what to do next. I came on this cruise with Kim because I felt totally lost. I hope by the end of it I will have somehow found my way."

"You will, Stevie. I suspect you already have." For a moment, he covered her hands that were clasped at his waist with one of his.

There was such compassion in his voice that

Stephanie felt a rush of warm emotion fill her. She felt faint and leaned into his back.

He was quiet for a moment and then told her, "I have to leave tomorrow. I just found out today my sous chef has Covid and I need to get back to run my trattoria. I apologize it is such short notice."

Stephanie's heart dropped. This was not how she thought the next few days might go. She held him tightly. "I'm so sorry."

They made the final climb to Taormina's stunning hilltop setting overlooking the Ionian Sea. Perched on a cliff and on the same ancient site for centuries, the medieval town bustled with activity.

Max drove to the edge of town and stopped at the Teatro Antico.

"This is what I want to show you, the Greek amphitheatre—still used today and so very special," Max said. "I know you are going to hike here with Kim, but I wanted the selfish pleasure of bringing you here first."

The stone columns and crumbling arches were haunting. Max told her that restoration was an ongoing undertaking and concerts and operas were regular events. An international festival was held there each summer.

He took a basket from a saddlebag on the bike. Holding Stevie's hand to help her over the uneven ground, he led her to a sheltered spot under some trees where they could sit. He spread a blanket and said, "Here's dinner. I prepared it this afternoon—and there is a small gift from Zio Emilio."

Stevie grinned at his thoughtfulness.

She was overwhelmed by the majesty of the ancient remains, still so very much intact. The breathtaking view beyond reached down to the cerulean sea. She touched her hand to heart. "Thank you for bringing me here. It is truly exceptional."

As the sun began to dip, shades of purple, pink and gold slowly blended in the sky in a dazzling display. Max took her hand and tenderly kissed her palm. "The beauty of this sunset cannot be adequately expressed in words. That's how I feel about you."

Stevie felt her heart flutter. She wanted this. She lifted his hand to her lips.

The moment hung in the air between them and then they smiled a little awkwardly. But their eyes held the message they were sharing.

Max poured them each a glass of wine from a small flask. "Just enough to go with dinner."

Then he said he had another question.

Stevie giggled. "I can't imagine what it will be this time."

"Will you let your hair down, StevieV? The way I'm used to seeing it in your videos?"

Now she laughed out loud. "I've been keeping it pulled back to stay incognito, hoping I wouldn't be recognized. I guess I've blown my cover."

Max watched as she undid the clasp holding her hair up. She gave her head a little shake as a riot of curls framed her head. She was surprised that she felt comfortable doing this and not clumsy which was her first thought when he asked.

They stared at each other. Stevie could feel something between them that was strong and good. She knew Max felt it too. Then he leaned forward. Suddenly he was running his fingers through her hair and drawing her gently to him.

He kissed her, softly at first. As Stephanie responded to his lips, he pulled her firmly against him and she willingly responded. The kiss became passionate and full of longing. Stephanie knew this was where she wanted to go. She felt found.

They embraced and covered each other's faces with kisses. After a while, they leaned against a tree trunk and watched the magnificent sunset, arms entwined, as they shared their innermost thoughts ... some serious, some frivolous. It was as if they each wanted the other to know who they really were.

In time they ate the delicious picnic. They began with a small bowl of seasoned olives, playfully feeding each other, along with a plate of anchovies marinated in lemon, garlic and oil.

Stephanie closed her eyes and sighed when she tasted them. "Divine," she said, her voice almost a whisper. Max's eyes crinkled with pleasure at her reaction.

Next, they had a Stromboli stuffed with sun-dried tomatoes, salami, ham and cheese, cut into wedges. "Pretty basic, but portable," Max said.

"Perfect," Stephanie assured him.

Then they shared a small ceramic bottle of limoncello sent by Emilio.

"Just enough for the final touch," Max said. "And from his farm."

They laughed and talked and kissed some more.

"*Dio mio*, I love kissing you," Max said. "And I don't want to stop there."

Stevie pressed her forehead into his chest and said, "Neither do I. But we have to. For now."

"Let's make a plan. Right now. Right here." Max said, weaving his fingers through hers and holding them tightly. Adding almost apologetically, "Am I rushing things?"

Stevie looked at him feeling love and trust. She knew because she felt so calm. Even though her tattoo was throbbing.

"Yes, you are," she said, "And it feels so right. Don't stop talking."

"You have two more ports of call before your ship arrives in Venice. In ten days. Let's talk every day. Then I will meet you there. In *La Serenissima*. I'll be the person that is pacing on the quay waiting just for you with the most enormous bouquet of roses you have ever seen. I will kiss you again—even more passionately. *Questo lo so*."

"And I will kiss you back even more passionately than that," Stephanie said. "This I know!"

They laughed and hugged and covered each other again with kisses as they promised this was the beginning and they would see where it went.

"My apartment is in an old palazzo with more rooms than anyone needs, tucked down a canal. Kim will be welcome to stay as long as she likes. As soon as you are ready, we will go on my bike to Marzabotta to make Paola's words come true. It's only a two-hour ride."

Stevie's heart soared. Everything was happening so

quickly and yet she felt no doubt about their plan. They would go to where it all began and from there she would start again, no longer lost.

The End

(but really—the beginning)

EPILOGUE

J anuary 2022

Max continued with his popular trattoria in Venice and Stevie could often be found in the kitchen beside him. They knew they were soulmates.

StevieV's Pasta Party on TikTok took on a new life and went viral.

Their first visit to Marzabotta was emotional. They met distant relatives of Stefano and discovered that the farm property on which he and Paola had lived for their brief time together was derelict. They visited the area several times, welcomed as *famiglia* and charmed by the pastoral atmosphere. Stephanie felt Paola's soul there as her tattoo thrummed gently.

When Stephanie first explained to her parents and Nonna Bella that she and Max were in love and wanted to marry and live in Venice, she was stunned by their response. During their three-month hiatus, they had been approached by Toronto real estate developers eager to purchase the Cara Mia property. Stephanie's desire to remain in Italy made their decision a simple one.

When her family came to Italy to visit with Stevie and Max, they all returned to Marzabotta together and a simple wedding was held in a field, under an arch of wildflowers. Kim was there to stand up for Stephanie. Max's and Chef Romano's large extended family and the distant relatives of Stefano held a feast that would never be forgotten.

As a wedding gift to the young couple, Stephanie's family bought them the long- abandoned farm property of Paola and Stefano.

Now drawings were under way for a home, next to the crumbled ruins that remained, with room for extended family to visit. Bella and the Angels promised they would return each year.

Stevie and Max worked on plans to establish an organic farm there to supply their restaurant and the local community.

A few months later, they were thrilled to share the news they were expecting a baby boy in the spring. They would name him Stefano.

Paola's words had come true. *"Sei il custode della nostra magia di famiglia"*.

The family magic would live on.

Dear Readers ~ If you enjoyed the day Stephanie and Kim spent in Antibes, you might want to read the six books in my bestselling series about Kat and Philippe's life that is set in that stunning part of the world. All the links can be found on <u>my website</u>.

If you enjoyed sailing away with Stephanie and Kim on The Dream Maker, you'll love cruising with Marie Stern on her trip in The Last Port of Call by Elizabeth Bromke.

★ <u>Don't miss a Sail Away book!</u> ★

(All the books are standalones and can be read in any order.)

Book 1: Welcome Aboard – prologue book
Book 2: The Sound of the Sea by Jessie Newton
Book 3: Uncharted Waters by Tammy L. Grace
Book 4: A Not So Distant Shore by Ev Bishop
Book 5: Caroline, Adrift by Kay Bratt
Book 6: Moonlight on the Lido Deck by Violet Howe
Book 7: The Winning Tickets by Judith Keim
Book 8: Lost At Sea by Patricia Sands
Book 9: The Last Port of Call by Elizabeth Bromke

ACKNOWLEDGMENTS

I hope you had as much fun reading this story as I had writing it! I've spent many years setting my stories on the sun-kissed shores of the Mediterranean, but taking you along on this cruise was a very different experience. I didn't want it to end!

If you enjoyed the day Stephanie and Kim spent in Antibes, you might want to read the six books in my bestselling series about Kat's unexpected mid-life journey that is set in the stunning south of France. All the links can be found on <u>my website</u>.

When I was first invited to join this awesome group of authors, I wasn't certain what my story would be about although there was never any question in my mind about the location. And then I remembered tales my good friend, Kimberly Lake, had regaled me with when she sold jewelry for a couple of years on a cruise ship. I can't thank her enough for all she shared with me.

The next thing I knew, the character of Stevie Valentini popped into my head and the two great friends were off on an adventure.

My thanks to my editor, Dinah Forbes, and to our cover designer, Elizabeth Mackey. As always, I am grateful to my advance readers. In particular, Gail Johnston, who has read this manuscript more times than anyone should ... and is still my dear friend. Also Patricia Caviglia, for her invaluable assistance with the Italian language ~ *grazie*.

My endless gratitude goes to a very special reader and truly a friend, whose name I borrowed (and slightly altered the spelling) for the character of Martha. Her wisdom, affection and kindness are my small tributes to the real person.

As always, I am grateful to Kerry Schafer, my Author Genie, who works her magic for me in so many ways.

A big bouquet of thanks goes to each author in this series for the wonderful sense of community that has existed through this past year as we each wrote our stories and worked together on how to bring this entertaining reading experience to booklovers everywhere.

Thank you for reading *Lost At Sea* and for telling your friends about the series. Thanks also for taking the time to leave short reviews which are so helpful to authors. I would love to have you sign up for my monthly newsletter (lots of giveaways, writing news, and always photos about my travels in France).

I hope you are swept away by all of the books in the series and then feel excited to explore the many great novels you see listed by each author. Once you finish this series, you're sailing into an endless sea of fabulous stories!

Happy reading!

About the Author

Patricia Sands lives two hours north of Toronto, but her heart's other home is the South of France. An avid traveler, she spends part of each year on the Cote d'Azur and once a year co-leads a 16-women, 12-day tour of the Riviera and Provence. Her award-winning 2010 debut novel, *The Bridge Club,* is a book club favorite. *The Promise of Provence,* which launched her three-part Love in Provence series was a finalist for a 2013 USA Best Book Award and a 2014 National Indie Excellence Award, an Amazon Hot New Release in April 2013, and a 2015 nominee for a #RBRT Golden Rose award in the category of romance.

Drawing Lessons, Sands' fifth novel, also set in the south of France, was released by Lake Union Publishing in 2017 and was a Finalist in the Somerset Literary Book Award 2019. The Villa des Violettes miniseries released in 2019/20 and she is currently working on Book 4 in the series.

A lifelong photographer, follow her to France on Instagram @psands.stories.

Find out more at Patricia's Facebook Author Page or her website where there are links to her books, social media, and monthly newsletter that has special giveaways and sneak peeks. She would love to hear from you!

www.patriciasandsauthor.com

facebook.com/AuthorPatriciaSands

instagram.com/psands.stories

goodreads.com/PatriciaSands

bookbub.com/authors/patricia-sands

www.ingramcontent.com/pod-product-compliance
Lightning Source LLC
Chambersburg PA
CBHW030629120726
47904CB00006B/2093